Everyone at the Central London Hospital agreed that the affair between Dr Nicola Lancaster and senior surgeon Andrew Ritchie was doomed from the start. Was there any chance that love might triumph in a surgical affair?

SURGEON'S AFFAIR

BY

ELIZABETH HARRISON

MILLS & BOON LIMITED
15–16 BROOK'S MEWS
LONDON W1A 1DR

First published in Great Britain 1985
by Mills & Boon Limited

©Elizabeth Harrison 1985

Australian copyright 1985
Philippine copyright 1985

ISBN 0 263 75097 3

Set in 10 on 11 pt Linotron Times
03–0885–57,500

Photoset by Rowland Phototypesetting Ltd
Bury St Edmunds, Suffolk
Made and printed in Great Britain by
Richard Clay (The Chaucer Press) Ltd,
Bungay, Suffolk

PRELUDE

One Night in Casualty

NICOLA was on call in Casualty that night. Workmanlike in a check cotton shirt, jeans and trainers, she walked across from the flat she shared with half a dozen others, enjoying the cool freshness of the night air after the heat of the day. A medical student in her fifth year at the Central London Hospital, she was hoping to qualify that autumn and become a surgeon like her father.

Small, slight, dark-haired, with brilliant blue eyes and a high forehead stuffed, her fellow students were given to complaining, with far too much brainpower for anyone so unfairly gifted with looks, she stood out even in the Central, where attractive girls were never in short supply.

As she reached the surgical block, a slim glass and steel tower, she saw Andrew Ritchie come out and cross the road. Disappointed, she watched his tall figure disappear. He must have finished for the day. She had been hoping that a difficult admission might have kept him in Casualty, but she was out of luck.

When she had been a first-year student in the medical school, Andrew Ritchie had been the demonstrator in anatomy, and he'd taught her the elements of surgery. Later, when she'd begun her clinical years, had started work in the hospital itself, she had encountered him again. He was Leo Rosenstein's registrar, assisting him in the theatre, accompanying him on the big teaching rounds. In addition, though, he took the students on rounds himself, and taught them, so that in fact they saw much more of him than of the consultant surgeons. It was then that Nicola had given him her heart. Somehow, when he was in the department, the air was alive with promise. She longed to be able to impress him with her ability, to make her mark as a potential surgeon.

Of course, she knew he was hardly aware of her existence, and this she accepted as a fact of life, just as she'd accepted her parents' divorce and the separation from her father. These things happened. But one could still dream. So Nicola allowed herself to dream about Andrew. Dreamt that she stood opposite him in the theatre, gowned and masked, assisting him, as she'd once imagined she might assist her father. Or he was a consultant, and she was his registrar, discussing the next day's list over coffee.

One day, she recognised, she'd look back at these student dreams of hers, laugh tolerantly, and wonder what had become of Andrew Ritchie, whom once she'd so much admired. In the meantime, though, he remained part of her daily life, and, idiotically, his tall frame filled her with confidence. It was ridiculous, but it happened. His rugged features, the blunt short nose, the wide mouth, the square chin with its deep cleft, were nothing special in themselves, she would remind herself as she studied him hungrily as he stood talking at the end of a bed. They just, ludicrously, turned her bones to water. Nothing could ever come of it, because, in addition to the awkward fact that he remained unaware of her existence, he happened to be well and truly married to another registrar.

However, while he was around there was no chance Nicola would lose her head over anyone else. Andrew Ritchie had immunized her against them all.

Tonight, she joined Giles Yorke in Casualty. Square and sturdy—though even he topped Nicola by a head – Giles was in his second pre-registration post. Nicola had known him for years—it had been Giles who had arranged for her to move into her present flat, round the corner from the hospital, where she had taken over his room when he went into residence.

The first patient to come Nicola's way was a middle-aged lady, a Mrs MacFarlane, who'd tripped over an uneven paving stone on her way back from bingo. She had cut her knee, and was also, in her own words, thoroughly shaken up.

'You can examine her, Nicky,' Giles said. 'Very thoroughly, to exclude any non-obvious injuries, and bearing in mind that we need to exclude fractures before we can send her home. We can't set to and X-ray her from head to foot, either, so what pictures—if any—we take will depend on what you find from your history and examination. If you want me for anything, I've a patient in the next cubicle.'

Mrs MacFarlane had no fractures, it turned out, and after Nicola had stitched the cut on her knee, she was able to go home. After this Giles told her to deal with a young night worker from the engineering machine shop with a cut arm. He was followed by the nightwatchman from the block of offices down the road from the hospital, who had cut his hand opening a tin of sardines for his three a.m. snack. And then an old friend, the mechanic from the all night garage at the end of Great St Anne's, came in with a load of dirt in his eye. He'd been working under a car, he explained, and the mud in the wheel arch had fallen over his face while he was trying to trace a fault in the lighting circuit.

She washed the eye out for him, checked that there was no evidence of corneal injury, and applied a pad and bandage. 'Leave this bandage on until the evening, and then if you come back we'll have a look at it.'

At that point Giles came in, looking for Nicola. 'Good lord, Dave, what are you doing here?' Giles owned an ancient Volkswagon Beetle, his pride and joy, which Dave somehow managed to keep on the road for him.

'Grit in me eye from a bloody wheel arch. But the lady's seen to it for me, and she reckons I'll live.'

'You'd better. Look, Nicky, if you've finished here,

there's a chap I want you to look at with me.' He led the
way to a cubicle further down the big hall.

The patient, a hefty man in a wheelchair, had been
brought in, Giles said, having injured his shoulder while
using his chain saw. 'Now stand square in front of him,'
Giles demanded, 'and tell me what you see.'

'This looks to me like the classic picture in Bailey &
Love of a dislocated right shoulder,' she said at once. It
had been easy.

'Right first time. I'll allow you to see the X-ray now.'
He pointed with his pen. 'See? So now what?' He shot
the question at her, imitating his chief on a teaching
round, although it was five in the morning.

'Reduction under anaesthetic?' Nicola knew this one.

'Providing,' Giles said warningly, 'there's no contra-
indication. Such as?'

'Bronchitis or a recent heavy meal.' Nicola was
prompt.

So was the patient. 'That's it, ducks,' he informed her.
'Had me breakfast, didn't I, before I started, at the caff
like I always does. Sausage, egg and chips. Me usual.'

'Therefore, what do we do now, would you advise?'
Giles had a triumphant gleam in his eye.

Why should he be looking so pleased? 'I know,'
Nicola began dubiously, 'it can be done without an
anaesthetic—wasn't it Hippocrates' own method?'

'That's right. And Kocher, don't forget him. Date?'

'About 1870.'

'Right. When I was on the orthopaedic side I saw this
quite often, of course, and I did two myself under
anaesthetic. So I feel just about ready to do one with the
patient awake.'

Now Nicola understood the air of concealed triumph.
There was nothing Giles enjoyed more than being in sole
charge. He had confidence in himself, justifiably, and he
liked to be in the driving seat. One of the joys of being on
at night, he'd often told her, was the opportunities you

were presented with. Your seniors were safely tucked up in their beds and only too eager to give you the go-ahead when you rang for their consent to act.

'Would you like to help me?' he was asking, his eyes shining in anticipation.

Nicola was almost as keen as he was. 'Rather.'

Giles' face fell. 'I suppose,' he said reluctantly, 'I'd better ring our Mr Ritchie to get his agreement.'

'I don't suppose he'll want to get up and come over,' Nicola said consolingly, though in fact her own spirits were soaring at the possibility that Andrew might after all appear in Casualty before the night was ended.

Giles was morose. 'You never know with him,' he said glumly. 'Too conscientious by half, he can be.' He made for the wall telephone, held the instrument while the ringing tone burred. He was sure he could do it. What he wasn't certain about was whether Andrew would see it his way. The knuckles of his hand tightened as an alert voice announced itself in his ear, as clipped and controlled as if it was mid-morning already.

'Ritchie.'

'Sorry to disturb you.' And that was the exact truth. 'But I thought I ought to consult you about a guy I've got here in Casualty with a dislocation of the right shoulder.' He went into details. 'Trouble is, he's had a heavy meal, but he's young and fit. I thought I could try a reduction without anaesthetic.'

'Hang on,' the metallic telephone voice said. 'Hold it a moment.' There was the briefest of pauses. 'I think I'll come over, Giles. Wait for me.'

'Hell.' Giles replaced the telephone disgustedly. 'Hardly a pause for thought, even. He's coming over. *Wait* for him. Wouldn't you know it? Doesn't he trust anyone?'

Nicola concealed her own surging delight. 'I expect he feels he ought to be around. After all, you haven't actually done it before, have you?'

Giles gave her an evil look. 'I told you, I've done it twice under anaesthetic. That gives you the feel of it all right. I *know* I could do it now. No problem.'

'I daresay you will. He only said to wait for him. I expect he just thinks he ought to be around while you do it.' Giles was enthusiastic and eager, which endeared him to patients, and often to his seniors, too. But not invariably. He was quick off the mark, and impulsive, Nicola had seen it for herself, and it was easy to imagine he might over-reach himself, take on a procedure with which he was not as much at home as he thought. This was how Andrew must be feeling now, she guessed, about Giles' ability to reduce the dislocation.

'Come on,' Giles was peremptory, his good humour entirely vanished. 'We'd better prepare the patient for sir.'

They were ready for Andrew when his tall figure came striding through Casualty, clad not in his usual suit but in jeans and a faded terracotta shirt.

Giles was politely welcoming, no sign now of his ill-temper. 'Sorry to have had to drag you out.'

'Where's the patient?'

'In here. On the couch ready for you. I've given him Diazepam 10 mg.'

'Right. Let's see him.'

The three of them entered the cubicle, Andrew standing aside for Nicola to precede him, something Giles would certainly never have thought of doing.

'Mr Ritchie has come in to advise me about this shoulder of yours,' Giles was telling the patient. 'He'll decide whether we should do it now, or wait until we can take you into the theatre.'

'I gather you've recently had a substantial meal,' Andrew commented.

'That's right. Sorry it's turned out so awkward, Doctor, but I always start the day with a good cooked breakfast inside of me. Heavy-like, me job is. No use trying to do it on a cuppa tea and a scrap of toast.'

'Using a chain saw, were you?'

'Yeah. Working on the demolition site round the corner, we are, and a bit be'ind schedule, so we've bin starting at first light, see? I was gettin' the props ready, and me saw hit back at me. Didn't like the early start, I daresay, no more nor what I do meself.'

'Bad luck. I'm just going to have a look at these X-rays, and then we'll see if we can get you back into proper working order.'

Giles' eyes lit up. Andrew was going to agree with him. He wasn't going to insist on waiting until the patient could be reduced under anaesthetic, he was going to allow him to do it here and now.

He had a rude awakening. After studying the X-rays and asking more questions, Andrew said 'You haven't actually done this before, have you, Giles?'

'Not without anaesthetic, no. But—'

'How often have you done it yourself in the theatre?'

'Twice,' Giles admitted. It was beginning to sound rather less impressive than when he'd been telling Nicola about it. 'But I've seen—'

'Have you seen it done with the patient awake?'

Giles knew then that he'd lost. 'Not actually, no.'

'Right. Well, now you can observe me, and next time we have one in you can do it, and I'll observe you. We'll use Hippocrates' method. Nicola, would you like to assist me, get the feel of it?'

Much more than she'd dared hope for. 'Please,' she breathed, her face as brilliant with joy as Giles' was loaded with gloom.

'We shall need our shoes off,' Andrew reminded her.

He was wearing trainers, like herself, Nicola noticed as she untied her own. Two people with trainers in common, like half the population, she told herself scornfully. She must be descending into lunacy to care like this.

'Now, what I want, Nicola, is for you to supply the strength and traction,' Andrew was explaining, 'because that's important. You need to find out exactly how much pull to exert. So you haul on the arm, while I guide your movements in the manipulation. I'm going to stand right behind you, like this.'

Suddenly he was there behind her, so close Nicola wanted to stand there for ever. And now his hands were gripping her arms, below the elbow.

She took a steadying breath, and with an effort looked at the patient's shoulder and somehow succeeded in concentrating on the job, instead of on Andrew.

'Do nothing unless I tell you,' he was saying. 'Right. Now put your right foot into his armpit. Yes. Take his elbow in your hand and exert a steady downward pull, parallel to the right side of his chest.'

'Like this?'

'Correct. At the same time, you must push him hard back with your foot, to stop him falling forward. Keep him steady, but go on pulling. Pull the arm, and push with your foot, and then we'll be ready for the manipulation, when your pulling has overcome the muscle spasm—that's the bit the anaesthetic would have done. You've got to haul much harder, you're being far too gentle. He's not going to break in two. You've got to have enough traction on the arm, as I said, to overcome the muscle spasm. So far you haven't, and until you manage it, we can't move further.'

Already Nicola was pink in the face from her efforts.

'Much harder,' the voice behind her repeated. 'So far you're not having any effect. Pull and push. Go on. *Harder*. You must haul on that arm with everything you've got.'

Nicola was purple in the face, now, her breath coming in great panting gasps.

Giles, watching, looked worried on her account, though inwardly he couldn't help being pleased at the certainty that he himself would have managed far better. If he'd been doing it, it would have been all over by now.

'Your traction is too weak to be effective, I'm afraid.' Andrew's voice was flat. 'We're getting nowhere. Let me take over.'

She couldn't bear it. She wasn't going to fail, surely? She wasn't going to be useless, was she?

'Stop hauling,' the inexorable voice behind her said. 'Let me take over. This unequal battle is ended, stat. Understood? I know you were doing your best, but it's not good enough, is it? Stand aside now.'

Nicola stood aside. Her best wasn't good enough.

Giles stepped forward eagerly. 'I can—'

Andrew put his own foot into the patient's armpit. 'I'll do it.' He was short. 'One training session is quite enough. A second would hardly be fair to our patient here.'

Even through her misery, Nicola could see that the patient, far from looking hard done by, was wearing an only too familiar expression—one of kindly male superiority. Very likely all three of them were enchanted she hadn't been able to make the grade. That would show her. Puny females like herself were useless in a real crisis.

Her fury, though, was directed mainly inward. She'd brought it all on herself. She'd been useless, no getting away from it. And just when Andrew Ritchie, of all people, had offered her this opportunity on a plate.

He was pulling the patient's arm down, just as she'd done. The difference was that he was able to go on from there, to the part of the manipulation she hadn't reached. He rotated the patient's wrist outwards, brought his arm across the front of his chest, there was a satisfying clunk, and the shoulder was back in its correct position. All this, it seemed to Nicola, in less time than it had taken her to position herself for action.

'Nothing to it, is there?' Andrew said to the patient,

now looking extremely surprised. 'But you need not only skill,' he added kindly, addressing Nicola, 'but also the requisite amount of strength. Not your fault you couldn't reduce it.'

Nicola felt like bursting into tears. Instead, methodically, she put her shoes back on.

Andrew did the same, chatting at the same time to Giles about new X-rays to make sure everything had returned to its place.

He swung round and addressed the patient. 'All right?'

'I'll say. Thanks, doc. It feels great to be back in one piece. Thought I was gonna be stuck like that for hours. Strewth, I'm glad they fetched you in.'

He was looking at Andrew, Nicola thought crossly, with an expression she understood only too well. Probably, without being aware of it, she looked at him like that herself. No doubt he was used to it, thought nothing of it.

'I'll just have a feel,' he said. His hands moved round the patient's shoulders. 'You're all right, I'd say, but you'll have to go back and have another X-ray, to be on the safe side. After that Mr Yorke here will strap your arm up for you. You won't be able to use your chain saw for quite a while.'

The patient looked mutinous.

'I mean that. It's important. If you don't rest your shoulder now, you'll put it out again before long, and each time you do that, the more likely it is to happen again.'

'Know where to come if I do, don't I?' The patient was bursting with good cheer and friendliness. 'I'll tell me mates, if they do anything like this, to make straight for the Central and you, doc. And Bob's y'r flip.'

'*Go slowly*,' Andrew said, unmoved. 'Don't get rash. If you put that shoulder out again, I'll leave you to Nicola here, so watch it.'

All three men fell about laughing.

Nicola flushed, though whether with rage or shame she had no idea.

'Well,' Andrew said, recovering, 'I'll leave him to you, Giles. X-ray him, strap him up, and keep on reading him the riot act.' He patted the patient lightly on his left arm above the elbow, remarking 'I'll see you again in Outpatients,' and left the cubicle.

Hastily, Nicola followed him. 'I'm awfully sorry,' she said urgently, 'to be so hopeless, I mean. I really did try, but I'm afraid—I suppose he was so massive, I just couldn't make any impression. I'm sorry.'

Andrew, who had been walking away towards reception, stopped in his tracks, so that Nicola almost shot past him. He looked her up and down. 'I told you, not your fault. Not a question of lack of skill, you merely didn't have the chance to exercise any skill, because of your lack of strength. Not to worry. Not thinking of going into orthopaedics, are you? If so, don't.'

'No, I know I'm not strapping enough for that. I'm sticking to general surgery.'

'You're *what*?'

'Sticking to general surgery,' she repeated, puzzled. Surely he'd grasped that she was dedicated to his specialty, all this time—nearly three whole weeks—that she'd been on his firm?

He hadn't, of course. Until this minute he'd never given it a thought. 'I assumed you were just putting in your stint,' he said slowly. His face had gone blank, whatever he was thinking hidden away, as if he'd been talking to an unsuspecting patient with a hopeless outlook. His swift glance swept over her again, up and down. Whatever he saw didn't appear to please him in any way, she thought dismally, as he continued to wear the off-putting blank expression. This worried her. With patients, no one wore an expression like this when it was good news. So he had bad news for her. He'd said, twice now, that her skill hadn't been at fault, though. So what could be wrong? She'd honestly imagined she'd done well during her three weeks. She enjoyed the work, she was neat-fingered and deft, and she knew her theory.

Her eyes searched his face with anguish.

Andrew was in a quandary. He ought to tell this silly girl not to waste her time. She'd be no more use in general surgery than she'd be in orthopaedics. Far too slight a frame, and weak-wristed, too. Why hadn't someone told her long ago?

She was good at the job, of course, as far as it went. But then that was to be expected. She was Rupert Lancaster's daughter. Amazing to think that vast brawny man had produced this waif of a girl. But why hadn't someone told her that surgery was not for her?

Presumably because she was Rupert Lancaster's daughter, and they assumed he'd tell her what lines her career should follow. Why hadn't he? Her parents had divorced, of course, and Rupert Lancaster had remarried—his theatre sister this time round, which was what, everyone had commented, he should have done in the first place.

'Have you talked to your father about your plans?'

Nicola was startled. She didn't know what she'd been expecting him to say, but it certainly wasn't this. 'No,' she said awkwardly. 'I—um—I don't actually see very much of him, you know. When I—when I'm not here, I usually stay with my mother and stepfather.'

'What does he do? Your stepfather?'

What an extraordinary conversation to be having in Casualty at six in the morning. 'He's a stockbroker.'

'Oh, not in medicine at all.' Hell, didn't she have anyone to advise her?

'No. I think that's why my mother married him, as a matter of fact. My father was so seldom at home, you see. My mother said marriage was for companionship, and bringing up a family together—and with my father there wasn't much chance of that.'

She was right there, Andrew thought. Rupert Lancaster was not what anyone meant by a family man. He was possessed by surgery, lived it and breathed it, and was ready, always, to give twenty-four hours of each day to his patients. Now this frail child thought she could follow in his footsteps, and no one had bothered to tell her the ambition was pointless.

Well, if no one had, in nearly five years, why should he have to be the one to break it to her? Why couldn't the dean of the medical school put her wise? Advising students was his job.

Blow that. The child was on his own firm, the subject had come up naturally—as it would have been bound to do, if not today, tomorrow or next week. It would undoubtedly have arisen sooner or later, because on the job her unsuitability made itself apparent. He ought to tell her now, this morning, while she was fresh from this particular failure, a failure that would demonstrate to her as nothing else could the inevitability of what he told her.

He straightened broad shoulders, the bleakness left his eyes and was replaced by a warm sympathy that reassured Nicola. Until he spoke. 'You have to face it, you know. Surgery is simply not on. Not for you.'

She went white.

Andrew was horrified. The poor kid really cared. So now what had he done?

'Not—not do surgery?' she repeated, a quiver in her voice and desolation in her eyes. 'You seriously mean—?'

'Yes, I do seriously mean.' He spoke harshly. Now he'd begun on this, he had to go through with it, but he hated what he was doing. It was proving much worse than he'd expected, but there could be no turning back now. What he was telling her was the truth, she'd have to face it sooner or later. 'You haven't the figure for it,' he said, in a vain attempt to lighten the mood.

So that was why he'd kept staring at her, looking her up and down like that. Because she hadn't the figure for a surgeon, and he'd seen it. The physical memory of how puny her efforts had been back there in the cubicle ten minutes ago gave absolute credibility to what he was saying, and she dared not argue. Only she couldn't just accept it without a murmur, take it or leave it, when it was, after all, her entire future going up the spout. Her entire life, come to that, that he'd just blithely jettisoned. 'I know,' she began with difficulty, 'that I was absolutely hopeless just now, but does that truly mean I can't think of surgery at all?'

'Eye surgery,' he said dismissively. 'Perhaps even neuro-surgery if you've the brains, which possibly you might have. But how are you going to get there, eh? Tell me that. Before you can specialise you'll have to do your house posts, and then put in for registrar's posts. You can't begin in the eye department as a pre-registration houseman, move across to neuro-surgery for your next pre-registration post, and then shuttle back and forth, and get the Fellowship. Incredibly narrow, and you'd be hopelessly handicapped in looking for a job at all, if the only thing you could take was in eyes, and you newly qualified. You'd spend months between posts hanging about unemployed, while everyone else was gaining experience, and you'd see yourself passed by people qualifying after you.'

Unfortunately, she could see he was right. Even so, she found she couldn't accept this sudden ending to all her hopes. She had to protest. Her intellect might tell her he was correct, but her jumbled emotions continued to pose what she half knew to be fruitless questions. 'But do I really have to decide, just like that, that all my plans were—were a mistake, that I—'

'Look,' he said. 'We can't stand here talking about it.'

He was fed up, and no wonder. He'd got out of bed and come across to Casualty to do a shoulder reduction, and here she was, pinning him against the wall outside the cubicle and demanding that he hold a seminar on her career plans at six in the morning. 'I'm so sorry, I—'

'Better come and have breakfast.'

Again it was the last thing she'd expected him to say. 'Br-breakfast?' she floundered, as if the meal was unknown to her.

'Breakfast,' he repeated patiently. The poor kid was shocked out of her mind. And he was the one who'd done it, even if it was in a good cause. He glanced at his watch. 'Not seven yet. So how about if you and I go off and have a smashing breakfast, and a good talk about your future?'

'Breakfast?' she said again, disbelievingly. Now he was sorry for her, that must be it, and so he thought he'd have to cart her off and fill her up with food. 'It's terribly kind of you, but you don't have to bother, honestly. I'm perfectly *all right*.' The final words spewed out vindictively, as if she was ready to bite him.

Andrew could gauge her reactions as easily as if she had been a patient in the ward. Low blood sugar. Getting emotional. He patted her, exactly as he'd patted the patient a quarter of an hour earlier, and replied with the utmost amiability, 'Of course you're all right, Nicola. Why on earth shouldn't you be? But it *is* about six-thirty, we do both of us need breakfast before we go to the wards, so come along, there's a good girl, and stop arguing.' He turned back towards reception again, and set off at a good pace.

Nicola, dazed, trod obediently two paces in the rear.

On the pavement he halted abruptly. 'Tell you what, we've a bit of time in hand. We'll drive up to Hampstead—it'll be much pleasanter there than it is down here, and we can have breakfast out of doors. How does that strike you?'

Nicola by now knew better than to argue with him—not that she wanted to. To go with Andrew to Hampstead for a meal—if she hadn't been so worried about her career she'd have been transported with joy. 'That'd be marvellous,' she told him. Her voice, though, failed to summon up any enthusiasm, came out tepidly.

Poor kid. Evidently he'd really delivered one below the belt. She was still thrown. It would be a good plan to get her away to Hampstead for a quiet meal with no interruptions and no probing eyes, so that they could have a serious discussion about her future.

'Come on,' he said, and led the way to his car, waiting in its space in the hospital parking area.

Driving with Andrew in his car to Hampstead for breakfast. Never had she supposed the day would dawn—but now it was so much dust and ashes. Not entirely dust and ashes, though. A small trickle of undoubted excitement joined the yawning desolation that had taken possession of her.

They left the car in a side street, and Andrew took her to a small restaurant halfway up the hill towards Jack Straw's Castle. Sam's Place, it was called, and they entered through an arched doorway that brought them into a small paved garden with a scattering of wrought iron tables and chairs, and a rampant Albertine rose in full spate climbing the house wall.

'Eat out here, shall we?' Andrew held a chair for Nicola. His tongue might often be abrasive, but his formal manners were punctilious, she thought.

'Be lovely. What a super place.'

They were joined promptly by the proprietor, a bald and tubby man wearing well-creased navy trousers, a white silk shirt with a navy and white spotted bow tie, and a blue-striped butcher's apron.

'Symphony in blue, this morning, I see,' Andrew commented, with a quizzical lift of his dark brows.

'The customers like the staff to be a bit posh-looking,

only not too much,' the owner explained with unimpaired good humour. He had, unexpectedly as far as Nicola was concerned, a rich Cockney accent.

'Bin on all night, 'ave yer?'

'Not me, no. I was only called out around dawn. But Nicola here's been on since midnight, so I've brought her to you for a proper breakfast.'

'Wot's it to be, then? Bacon and egg, or y'can 'ave kidneys—oh no, I forgot. Don't like them, do yer? Leo won't touch 'em, either. Sausage and egg, and seein' as it's you, I'll throw in a rasher of best back as well, or you can 'ave an omelette. Plain or mushroom, and I'll throw in the rasher with that, too. Or scrambled eggs, I can do, if you'd prefer.'

Nicola's eyes glazed, and not from lack of sleep.

'Sam makes a fantastic omelette,' Andrew informed her. 'I recommend that, as it's on offer.'

'Thank you, that'd be great.'

'Don't do omelettes for everyone, not at breakfast,' Sam said. 'But the rush don't begin until nearly nine, and me busy time's around nine-thirty to ten-thirty.' He shrugged. 'There y'are, that's 'Ampstead for yer. Mushroom omelettes, then, and a big pot o' coffee, right?'

'And some hot rolls, and some of your blackcurrant jam.'

'Right. Back in a tick.'

'Sam was at school with Leo,' Andrew said, as if this explained everything—as indeed it did. Leo Rosenstein, the consultant surgeon who was their chief, was a rollicking character with a voice like a foghorn, an acute and penetrating mind, clinical acumen and diagnostic flair envied even by the department of medicine, and an international reputation as a surgeon. He was outspoken, overbearing, enormous fun to be with, and his friends extended from the back streets of London to the far corners of the globe.

Sam was back before Nicola would have believed it possible, with a glass pot of coffee, a jug of cream, a wicker basket of rolls and a dish of blackcurrant jam. 'Just gonna do y'r omelettes,' he announced, setting everything down and departing at speed.

'You get much quicker service here than in any canteen,' Andrew said. 'Would you like to pour?'

She lifted the pot, poured a dark and fragrant steaming liquid into big pottery cups striped in blue and maroon. Sitting in a garden in Hampstead, in a restaurant owned by a friend of Leo Rosenstein's, pouring coffee for Andrew Ritchie. If she'd suspected last night that this was what the morning would bring, she would have been out of her mind with excited anticipation. And now here she was, and all she could remember was that Andrew had said she must give up all idea of surgery.

Well, she told herself firmly, to be here with him on this early summer morning was not a bad beginning to a new life, and she had better make up her mind to enjoy it. It was, after all, likely to be the only occasion on which she would sit at a little wrought iron table under a cloud of Albertine roses having breakfast with Andrew.

Sam was back, with two enticing omelettes, oozing their filling on to a scalding plate, accompanied by not one but two of the promised rashers, crisp and curling. The aroma of perfectly grilled bacon joined that of the coffee and the roses, and Nicola suddenly found not only that she was ravenous, but that she seemed to be enjoying herself after all.

As they were finishing the omelettes, and talking about another hot roll with the blackcurrant jam—apparently also made by Sam—he was back. 'Ow about a nice bowl of fresh raspberries, to round it off, eh?'

'Wow,' Nicola exclaimed.

Andrew grinned. 'You may take it the lady would like some raspberries, Sam. And so would I.'

Two brimming bowls of fresh raspberries arrived, and brought yet another fragrance to what was undoubtedly, Nicola felt, the breakfast of the century. Sam assessed their supplies. 'Cream you've got. Sugar, too. Another pot of coffee, shall I bring? Or 'ow about a nice glass of white wine to go with the fruit?'

'Hold it, Sam. You can't send us back to the hospital sloshed at this hour.'

'One glass of wine isn't goin' to do no one no 'arm.'

'Nicola?'

She could only gaze wide-eyed. 'W-wine for breakfast?' she enquired faintly.

'Nothin' wrong with that,' Sam told her. 'Wot about Buck's Fizz, eh? Bet you've 'ad that and thought nothing of it.'

'Well, no, actually I haven't.' She was apologetic, feeling she was failing to match up to the expected standard of Sam's customers. Perhaps Leo had Buck's Fizz every morning, as a matter of course. 'I've heard about it, but I've never had it.'

'Then,' Sam said triumphantly, 'you'd certainly better 'ave the wine now. Time you learnt to 'ave a touch of alcohol with y'r breakfast when you've bin up all night.' He cast a rapid glance gowards Andrew, who nodded.

'I'll get it,' Sam said. He returned with the speed of light, bearing two tall glasses of a chilled white wine from the Moselle that went perfectly with the raspberries. Nicola sipped, took a mouthful of fruit, sipped again, and looked across at Andrew. 'I've never had a breakfast like this in my life,' she said.

Andrew was touched. She was a sweet child. Attractive, too. A pity he'd had to demolish her hopes for the future.

'Sorry about having to bring you down to earth about your career, though,' he said. 'But it would be a grave error for you to pin your hopes on surgery, as I said. You'd have every chance of doing well in some other

speciality, whereas in surgery you could never be anything other than second-rate. You haven't the strength.
Possibly not the stamina, either. But certainly not the
weight, as evidenced by this morning. How much do you
weigh? Somewhere around 112 lbs?'

She nodded. 'A bit less, if anything.' Why had it never
occurred to her that her small frame and lack of pound-
age would interfere with her surgical capabilities? Why
couldn't someone have told her sooner?

'And look at these wrists of yours,' Andrew was
continuing. He took one of her wrists in his hand, turned
it over disparagingly. 'Chicken bones,' he said, and
dumped her hand unflatteringly back again on her side
of the table.

This was not what had happened in Nicola's dreams
when Andrew Ritchie had taken her hand across a table
in a restaurant. She drank some wine, frowned, and
decided she ought to put up at least an imitation of being
a keen and receptive student. 'I'm sure you must be
right,' she told him. 'It's just that it's a bit difficult to
readjust. You see, I've never thought of doing anything
else but surgery, and—'

'Because of your father, would that be?'

'I suppose it must have been. And then, apart from
that, as soon as I came into the theatre, I—well, it
sounds quite mad, I suppose, but I sort of felt at home
there, as if I belonged.'

'It doesn't sound mad to me. It was exactly how I felt
myself, from the very first day.'

'It was?' Nicola's eyes took fire, and burnt with a deep
blue light.

Andrew had never seen this before. He was fascinated. He stared back at her.

To Nicola he seemed to be looking straight through
into her soul. Alarmed at what he might find there, she
dropped her gaze hastily, and carefully spooned up her
raspberries.

Disappointed, Andrew drank the last of his wine, and returned to the subject of her career. 'If you like it there, why not settle for one of the other jobs in the theatre? How about anaesthetics, for instance? You'd be part of the surgical team—an essential part of it, no doubt about that. You'd be there looking after the patient all the time. Plenty of responsibility, too. After all, it's the anaesthetist who's in charge of the patient throughout— if he says stop, the patient's not up to it, the surgeon stops.'

Nicola was past all thought. She'd never before considered doing anaesthetics, she wasn't immensely taken with the idea, since she hadn't yet truly relinquished the picture of herself as a surgeon. At this particular moment, though, she was high on Sam's restaurant, Hampstead, raspberries, white wine and, most of all, Andrew's company. If he had advocated hurling herself off the top of the surgical block at the Central in order to further her career, she'd very likely have done exactly that. All she said was, 'It would mean working in the theatre, that's true.'

Andrew wanted to see her forging ahead on new lines. The sooner she adapted to a change in direction the better for her. Nothing to be gained by sitting about regretting a forsaken path. 'How about if I have a word with Chasemore, ask him to have a talk to you?' he enquired.

Nicola was startled. Robert Chasemore was the consultant anaesthetist in general surgery, and director of the intensive care unit. He had a world-wide reputation and, as far as Nicola was concerned, was both eminent and forbidding. The possibility of discussing her career prospects with him would never have crossed her mind. 'Do you think he would?' she asked doubtfully.

'Sure of it. That's settled, then. I'll have a word with him today.'

'Th-thank you.' Events were moving fast, and Nicola

with them. Last night her dreams had consisted of herself as a qualified surgeon, assisting Andrew in the operating theatre. Now her hopes of a future in surgery had been dashed, while her dreams of Andrew had become this reality of sitting here in Hampstead opposite him, having breakfast with raspberries and wine. Totally different, but far better than anything dreamed up in her imagination. She smiled at him with her heart in her eyes.

He was jolted. He'd never seen anything like these eyes of Nicola's. A moment ago all blue fire, but now liquid like the waters of heaven. He could drown in them for ever and a day.

Abruptly he stood up. 'Time we were getting back. I'll just see Sam, and we'll be off. Wait for me.' He departed through the little garden and into the restaurant itself with the familiar long-legged stride, that until this morning Nicola had seen only around the hospital.

CHAPTER ONE

Working at the Central

ANDREW was a fast-mover. Nicola's appointment with Robert Chasemore, the anaesthetist, was fixed for the following day. Before she had even grown used to the idea, her new career was launched. When she qualified that autumn, her first pre-registration post was as his house physician. Next she landed a coveted post, that of house physician to the professor of medicine—a job given only, they said at the Central, to highbrows. After this, fully qualified and on the medical register, she returned to the department of anaesthetics.

She continued to do well. She had a post as senior house officer in the department of medicine, and then became anaesthetic registrar in accident and emergency, and more recently she'd become Robert Chasemore's registrar. She'd taken the Membership of the Royal College of Physicians, and gained it at her first attempt— the professor of medicine would probably have scalped her if she'd failed. Even so, the achievement was a minor triumph, and awed her contemporaries.

She had her own small flat now, in the block owned by the hospital overlooking St Anne's Square. Undoubtedly, as far as the outside world was concerned, she had it made. Cool, laid-back and competent, that was Nicola Lancaster, they said around the Central. A looker, too, with that petite but undeniably ravishing figure—her legs were the sort that ought to be insured, they often added—and the brilliant blue eyes under arched brows. She had not married, of course, but then none of them had expected her to. Cool, after all, was the significant word. She was far too busy climbing the career ladder to contemplate marriage.

She encouraged this attitude, keeping her inconveniently enduring feeling for Andrew Ritchie to herself, and trusting that as the years went steadily by she'd come to her senses, find she was over him.

The passing years had not treated him altogether kindly. True, exactly as they'd predicted, he'd achieved his consultant post in general surgery. But his marriage had failed. His wife, who had been awarded a year's fellowship at the Johns Hopkins in the USA, had never returned to the Central. Instead, she'd accepted a highly paid post in Saudi Arabia. Since Andrew had no intention of joining her there, and Gillian Ritchie declared that nothing would induce her to come back to the hard grind and low pay of London hospitals, they agreed to divorce. Their marriage hadn't worked out, owing to the demands of differing careers, but they remained good friends, though leading separate lives.

So Andrew Ritchie was a bachelor again, and the female side of the hospital rejoiced, preparing to demonstrate to him daily—even hourly—that Gillian was untypical, that the Central was stacked to the rafters with girls longing to devote themselves to him for ever. He'd always been in demand, though not as goodlooking, purists asserted, as many of the Central consultants—indeed, there were those who argued that his strong-boned face missed downright ugliness by a mere fraction. However, he had something extra, most of them agreed. He just happened to be a knock-out. As he arrived for the ward round, his broad-shouldered bulk reassured staff and patients alike. He brought a sense of comfort, a feeling that all would be well.

Admiring hordes of yearning girls were ready, wherever Andrew went in the hospital, with cups of tea or coffee, Horlicks or cocoa in the small hours, biros for signing forms, rubber gloves and gowns for donning, cloths for wiping the brow in surgery, or, the ultimate ambition of course, their bodies to use as he liked.

Nicola might secretly share this ambition, but she made sure no one guessed it. She saw him daily now, exactly as she'd imagined in her student years, working alongside him in the operating theatre. The relationship between them was strictly professional, and she was thankful for it. Or so, at any rate, she informed herself. His advice about her choice of career had been good. She owed her success to his interference at a crucial stage.

Anaesthetics suited her. She enjoyed her job—meeting patients in the ward before their surgery, reassuring them about the coming operation, planning the right anaesthetic for them, seeing them through the surgery and back into the recovery room. She liked looking after the dangerously ill patients in intensive care, knowing that it was her skill that could put them on their feet again. Most of all, of course, she enjoyed working with Andrew, being able at last to take his presence for granted. Except that this was something she never did. To be with Andrew—in the ward, the operating theatre, or simply planning tomorrow's list over a cup of coffee—remained her personal notion of heaven.

This morning was his operating list, and soon after seven Nicola walked round St Anne's Square and into the surgical block, her spirits soaring. In the lift, zooming silently up the tower block to the general theatre suites, she smiled to herself at the prospect of the day ahead, a trim, neat girl in a white linen skirt with a navy shirt that darkened her eyes to magical depths of colour. The lift doors opened, she stepped briskly through them and along the corridor towards whatever the day might bring.

She went straight to the changing rooms, and by seven-thirty, gowned but, for the patient's benefit, not yet masked, though her dark hair was already pushed back into her cap, she entered the anaesthetic room to prepare the first patient, a Mr Thornbury, whom she'd seen in the ward the previous afternoon.

Mr Thornbury had had his pre-medication an hour ago, but he seemed wide awake and alert. As soon as he saw her come in, he raised himself on his elbow. 'Good morning, Dr Lancaster.' A driving, successful man in his fifties, he had suffered for years from a peptic ulcer that, as he'd done his best to ignore it, had troubled him more and more. Now he'd reached the stage where he'd at last come round to consulting his family doctor, who had promptly sent him to a general physician in Harley Street, who in his turn had referred him to Andrew. What they were all afraid of was that a malignant change might have occurred. That Mr Thornbury had not only ulcers but a cancerous growth.

This morning they were to open him up and find out. The operation, at the beginning of the list, was booked as a laparotomy, meaning simply that they were uncertain what they were going to find. The operation was exploratory, in order to discover the cause of the blockage at the exit from the patient's stomach that made him vomit his food back at the end of a meal. Once it was found, Andrew was hoping to be able to relieve the obstruction and open the exit from the stomach again.

'How much time is this little job going to take?' Mr Thornbury asked. He was, they'd already noticed, a split-second merchant, and insisted on regarding his approaching operation as if it were no more than a quick visit to the dentist for a filling. Nicola and Andrew had connived at this attitude of his, feeling that the pretence was Mr Thornbury's own method of keeping up his morale. 'I've a telephone call from Geneva coming through at one-thirty,' he was saying. 'I've told them to put it through to me here at the hospital—I don't want to have to leave it to my deputy. I'll be back in my room and ready to take it by then, won't I?' He glared at her, as if by exerting enough pressure he could force her to rush the anaesthetic and hurry them along in the theatre, too.

'I'd better be,' he added. This was how he had run his business for years. What worked there should also work in the Central London Hospital, he'd decided.

Nicola knew, of course, that what lay ahead of him might be a simple and comparatively quick operation, or it could involve the removal of a major part of his stomach, followed by the reconnection of the healthy portions both above and below the part they'd removed. Mr Thornbury might imagine he was tough, could stand up to anything, but now didn't seem exactly the moment to impart these facts to him. Her face remained unreadable. Her years of training saw to that. What was needed at this juncture, even though Mr Thornbury didn't suspect it, was reassurance. She smiled down at him. 'A full diary, even on the day of your operation, Mr Thornbury?' she enquired lightly. 'We don't have many patients like you, I must say.' And praise the lord for that, she was thinking, though she was schooled not to allow this antagonistic reaction to colour her voice, into which she tried to force admiration.

It came off. He was pleased. Gratified, too. 'Ha,' he said. 'That's why our turnover last year was over two million, Doctor. And this year already we're heading for two and a half.'

The nurse who'd brought him up from the ward raised eyes heavenwards.

'Well, the sooner we get on with this, Mr Thornbury, the sooner you'll be back to take your call,' Nicola told him cheerfully.

'Suits me. Let's go.' He was full of confidence now. He'd made his mark. This pretty little doctor wouldn't forget what he'd said in a hurry, and she'd pass it on to them in the theatre, he was sure of it. After all, she'd been impressed, he'd seen that for himself.

Nicola was reaching for the syringe containing the intravenous anaesthetic she had ready. She injected it, and by the time the light over the automatic doors glowed green, indicating that the theatre was ready for the first case on the list, Mr Thornbury was well under. He was wheeled through, a mask over his face now, a tube connecting it with the anaesthetic machine. Nicola supported his head, with the mask, while the others, under her supervision, lifted him across from the trolley on to the table, moving him with infinite care so as to make sure he could suffer no injury—his limbs limp and flaccid under the anaesthetic, he was helpless. As soon as he was satisfactorily positioned on the table, Nicola began arranging his right arm on a support, so that she could give injections into his vein, or put up a drip-transfusion should it prove necessary. As she was finishing, Andrew, masked and gowned, gloved hands raised, joined them at the table.

'Morning, everyone. Hullo, Nicola, how's it going?'

'Fine. He's deep enough for you to go straight ahead. He was on until the last moment, would you believe, about a telephone call he seems to be expecting from Geneva at lunch time.'

'Better keep our fingers crossed about that.' Andrew sounded grim. Like them all, he hated opening a patient up to find a spreading malignant growth. 'We may need to do a partial gastrectomy, Sister, though I hope he may get away with simply a by-pass.'

As usual, Stella Jarvis was unperturbed. 'I have the gastrectomy trolley prepared, Mr Ritchie.'

However, it turned out, to everyone's relief, that Mr Thornbury was not after all going to need this trolley. There was no malignant growth in his stomach, what had happened was simply that the years of ignoring his peptic ulcers while they waxed and waned had resulted in scarring of the outlet from his stomach, so that his meals, not able to pass onwards, had been regurgitated. Andrew explained this to the students in the gallery. 'See?' he demonstrated. 'You can hardly pass a finger through it.' To the group round the table with him, he added in a lower voice, 'Let alone one of Mr Thornbury's full-scale expense-account meals.' He raised his voice again. 'So now we'll set to and make a new opening from the stomach into the upper intestine, to allow the stomach to empty normally, and I reckon he'll feel a new man as a result.' This was the sort of experience that made him glad to be a surgeon.

Nearly an hour later, Nicola took Mr Thornbury through into the recovery room. Within half an hour he was able to return to the ward and await his Geneva call.

Long before this, Nicola had returned to the anaesthetic room, where her immediate junior, the anaesthetic house physician—a slight, fair boy called Neil—was already talking to the next patient, who was to have an appendicectomy. On the previous evening, when they'd been arranging the list, they had agreed that as they were not sure how long Mr Thornbury's operation would take, nor what state he'd be in when he went to recovery, whether Nicola would need to stay with him, Neil would carry on and give the gas for the appendicectomy, a straightforward case. She remembered Giles and Andrew in her student days, and knew that Neil was going to be disappointed to see her quick arrival, before he'd had a chance to administer the anaesthetic himself.

'This is your case, Neil,' she said. 'So go ahead—don't mind me. I'm going to write up my notes.' She went over to the side table to enter up Mr Thornbury's operation details in the anaesthetic record, and to be at hand if she was needed.

Five minutes later, Neil had induced a perfect state of anaesthesia, and the patient was deeply asleep. 'He's all yours,' Nicola said. 'I'll play no part unless you need me. Don't mind asking, though.' She went through with Neil and the appendicectomy patient, back into the operating theatre.

'Morning, Neil,' Andrew greeted him at once. 'You and Jeremy are doing this case, we decided, didn't we?'

Jeremy Moorcroft was Andrew's registrar—Giles Yorke's successor, as it happened. 'Nicola and I will be here if you want us, either of you. But pretend you're on your own—unless, that is, you find something startling and need some help.' He stepped back from the table. To have your chief breathing down your neck as you operated, though sometimes essential, was apt to be unnerving.

He turned to Nicola. 'Chasemore's doing the gas for the next case—the renal calculus—isn't he?'

Nicola nodded, moving at his side into the scrubbing up and gowning bay. 'That's right. I'll be there too, though, as Mr Thornbury isn't going to need me in recovery. I want to watch my astounding chief get a frail patient like Mrs Bentley safely through a major operation. When two of our visitors in the gallery have taken the trouble to fly in from Switzerland to see Robert Chasemore give a general anaesthetic on a dodgy patient, I certainly intend to be there at his side, keeping my beady eye on his every move.'

'You'll be there for the rest of the list, then.' Andrew sounded pleased. 'Afterwards perhaps we could have lunch?'

'I'd love that.' The casual phrase was no more than the exact truth.

Lunch was delayed, the renal surgery proving long and involved, but they were able to go off together at last, soon after two in the afternoon, to Giovanni's, the little Italian restaurant just along the road from the hospital. Nicola often went there with Andrew— but always, as was the case today, for a quick bite after a long surgical list, or perhaps a snack after a lengthy round. They didn't even bother to go upstairs. Upstairs was more formal, for celebrations or pundits. Andrew, of course, was a pundit these days, but when he was in a hurry he usually ate downstairs with the mob.

Nicola had been upstairs, but not often, and only in a

group. They had in fact celebrated her acquisition of
the Membership there, in a party hosted by Robert
Chasemore himself. On another occasion she'd been
upstairs to celebrate Giles' appointment as a senior
registrar at St Mark's, Halchester. Apart from herself, the party had been entirely surgical, and once
again included Andrew, with Leo Rosenstein, Sister
Henderson and Nick Waring, another general surgeon,
with his wife Sophie.

That was how it went. Either she was with Andrew in a
huge group, or, if she had him to herself, it was for a
routine snack, like today.

They ate sea-food pasta, with a green salad, and
discussed the morning's surgery from start to finish in
enormous detail. After this they had strawberries and
cream, and talked about patients in the ward, pre- and
post-operative. And then they returned to the hospital,
after, Nicola thought a little wearily, another useful
working lunch, such as Andrew might have had with any
colleague. While she remained besotted by him, he
didn't know she existed, other than as a pair of hands or
a trained mind. So what she ought to do, and before too
long, was call it a day. Take a post somewhere else.
Make a new life for herself, without Andrew, or any
thought of him.

Easier said than done.

'You know,' he remarked suddenly, as they were
walking back, 'we only ever seem to have these hurried
meals between appointments. No time to talk, to un-
wind. Why don't we go out one evening for a decent
meal somewhere, take our time for once, forget the
hospital?'

Had he read her mind? Terrified of sounding child-
ishly over-eager for this heavenly opportunity,
Nicola accepted in an off-hand manner that more than
concealed her delight. She sounded as though she might
easily overlook the date, forget to turn up. No one, least

of all Andrew, could have guessed the nail-biting anticipation she endured for the rest of that week. To her infinite relief, when the evening actually arrived, Andrew wasn't called to the theatre for an emergency, she wasn't kept late in intensive care. Neither of them had to telephone at the last moment cancelling everything. Her only problem, it turned out, was to find something suitable to wear.

She didn't want to look too dressed up—as if the chance of an evening with Andrew had gone to her head, and made her outfit herself as if for a banquet at Buckingham Palace or Hampton Court. On the other hand, she didn't want to seem casual and uncaring, appear in her ordinary hospital gear, when he'd taken the trouble to book a table at an expensive restaurant. She scowled at all her clothes, finally settling on a long-sleeved shirt-dress in a Liberty silk, that she'd bought precisely because it would go anywhere. A most useful dress. A dress for committees or cocktail parties, for dinner with Robert Chasemore, for sherry in the boardroom with eminent overseas visitors, or even for a quiet evening in her own flat with a few friends. A dress, too, she could safely wear in the hospital without eliciting wolf whistles in the lift if she had to go over around midnight to intensive care. It might fit like a glove, but it was high-necked and long-sleeved, and no one could peer down her front.

Unbearably prim, it made her look like the worst sort of woman doctor, sexless, rigidly professional, she decided, her spirits collapsing as she examined herself in her looking glass. Why on earth had she ever bought it? She couldn't possibly go out with Andrew in it.

Her door bell rang.

He had arrived.

She'd have to stay in this bloody dress.

She let him in, offered a drink.

'Better be on our way, perhaps. I booked a table for

eight o'clock, and we may have difficulty parking.'

He didn't intend to waste a second, she saw. A quick meal, and back to the hospital. Perhaps she was wearing the right dress, after all. A business-like dress, suitable not only for Robert Chasemore, but Andrew Ritchie, too.

He took her to the Country Garden, a small restaurant much favoured by Central consultants, which until now Nicola had known only by reputation. Quite different from Giovanni's, it was off the beaten track, quiet and unostentatious, with a charm all its own. Gingham curtains shrouded lattice windows, pine dressers held flowery china, while the superb food, she was to discover, arrived on the same china. They ate in a small quarry-tiled dining room looking out on to a tiny ivy-grown patio with an urn, and Nicola thought she had never been so happy in her life.

Andrew watched her, waiting for the sudden gleam of blue light as her eyes met his. This phenomenon had fascinated him since that morning five years ago in Hampstead, though he'd done his utmost to put it out of his mind. With one unsuccessful marriage behind him, the last thing he wanted was a relationship with another careerist woman doctor.

So what the hell was he doing here tonight?

He sighed. He'd managed to withstand Nicola's lure for years, reminding himself regularly that drowning for ever in the pools of her disturbing eyes was not for him. He was fond of her, that was all. She was a nice girl, and she'd become a good, capable doctor. He'd been able to help her with her training, to influence her towards a change of course that had done her nothing but good. From then on, naturally, he'd taken a mild, elder-brotherly sort of interest in her progress. His was the helping hand that father of hers had neglected to provide.

Yet for over a year now, he'd found himself looking

forward to entering the operating theatre, knowing she'd be there at the patient's head, that above her mask those amazing eyes would meet his, and the list would have begun. He was hungry, each morning, for her company.

The knowledge terrified him. Gillian's defection had hit him hard, and he'd reacted not only with anger but with cynicism. So much for love and marriage. So much for career women. Never again would he confuse sex with marriage, or even with loving and caring. Any loving and caring would be kept for patients.

In any case, to have an affair with Nicola would never do. General surgery would watch every move they made, speculating and gossiping, waiting for some fascinating denouement. They'd lay bets on whether he'd taken Nicola to bed, whether he had marriage in mind. They'd all been distressed, he'd known it at the time and it hadn't made his position any easier, at the break-up of his marriage to Gillian, and he was well aware that they were eager to see him satisfactorily settled again.

They were not going to have the opportunity to watch him start any kind of an affair with Nicola. She was far too vulnerable. Those looks she gave from her witch's eyes said more than she meant him to know. She was his for the taking. But he had no intention of marrying again. Once was enough. More than enough. And to have a passing affair with Nicola was out of the question.

Delightful, though.

Why should he assume it would be so hard on her? It could easily be an enjoyable and thoroughly rewarding experience for them both. Damn it, he'd make sure she enjoyed it, if nothing else. So why hesitate? Was it true that she was so hopelessly vulnerable? In this day and age?

She was a career girl, everyone said that. She wasn't looking for marriage. So why not have a delightful, light-hearted affair with her?

'More coffee? Or shall we be going?' he asked abruptly, glancing at his watch. 'I ought to go in and see that bronchitic we did the hernia on.'

'Of course,' she said at once. 'I want to look in on intensive care myself, in any case.'

'Back to the grindstone,' he said, with a somewhat lopsided grin she was at a loss to comprehend.

She sat beside him in the Porsche he'd recently acquired, and they drove back to the Central car park. It was over. Finished. One blissful evening at the Country Garden with Andrew, gone like a flash. Over. And once again, as usual, they'd talked about patients, about hospital problems. Never about anything personal.

To wear the Liberty shirt-waister had been right. Because here she was, exactly as she'd foreseen when she bought it, wearing it to go into intensive care. It was a most suitable dress. For a busy woman doctor with no sex life.

What she hadn't bargained for, though she might, knowing the Central, have expected it, was that she and Andrew had been spotted. Sister Theatre—no longer Barbie Henderson, who'd finally accepted an overdue higher administrative post, but the beautiful West Indian, Stella Jarvis, who had a flat in Nicola's block— had seen her getting into the Porsche with Andrew. The news went round like a prairie fire.

Even Giles, down at Halchester, heard it on the grapevine before the week was out, and took it on himself, when he came up to London for a lecture at the Royal College of Surgeons, to seek Nicola out and warn her against any involvement with Andrew.

'Listen, sweetie, he's not looking for permanence,' he pointed out over a mound of pasta—he'd carted her off to Giovanni's for a quick meal before his train left. 'He's not going to settle down again. It went too wrong with Gillian, and he's through with marriage.'

'Hold it, Giles. We had one meal at the Country Garden a week ago. Who said anything about marriage?'

'Just as long as you aren't kidding yourself, duckie.' He eyed her uneasily.

He was right, of course. He'd known her for ever, and he saw much she'd prefer to keep hidden.

'Steer clear of Andrew, Nicky. You're not in his league. If you get involved with him, you'll be hurt.'

'I can look after myself, thank you very much.'

Giles ignored this meaningless remark. 'Anyway,' he added, reassuring himself but not Nicola, 'I don't suppose for a minute he'd ever think of you as a girl friend, so don't expect too much, will you, simply because for once he took you to the Country Garden? Don't assume he's leading up to anything. Not with you.'

'Great. Thanks very much.'

'I don't mean he wouldn't find you attractive,' he assured her hurriedly. 'Anyone would. You're a dish. All the men say so.'

All except Andrew, that was.

'But don't imagine Andrew will get serious about you, that's all,' Giles went on. 'Andrew Ritchie does have some principles, after all.'

'Principles?' Now he'd really lost her. 'What on earth about, you lunatic? Why should he suddenly have principles about me? What's supposed to be so special about me?'

To her rage, Giles spelled it out to her. Andrew was a responsible consultant, who'd known her throughout her student days, who'd taught her himself. He wouldn't so much as consider making love to her unless he was serious and intended marriage. 'Which we all know he doesn't.'

To Giles and Andrew both, apparently, Nicola Lancaster was not for fun and games. Only for marriage. Was she wearing a label, or what?

'Come off it, Giles. Try living in today's world for a change. You may think about me like that, though I can't imagine why you should, but no one else does. Wake up.'

Back in her own flat that evening, though, when she thought over what Giles had said, she came reluctantly to the conclusion that just possibly he could be right. If, that was, there was the faintest chance of Andrew being interested in her at all as a female—which she rather doubted—he might well hold back. For all the reasons Giles had so maddeningly listed. His principles. His seniority. His sense of responsibility.

She saw very clearly, inescapably, where this new understanding led her. If the undemanding friendship she and Andrew had now was ever to move into something more exciting, she was the one who'd have to bring it about. No good waiting for Andrew, held fast in his principles and all the rest of it. In the past Andrew had set the pace, while she hung longingly around, grateful for any crumb. That would have to stop. She'd have to take matters into her own hands, otherwise nothing would happen between them, ever.

Look at it, she told herself, dispassionately. As if she could. But at least she'd try. That first breakfast in Hampstead, for instance. She'd certainly never expected it to lead anywhere—other than to an appointment with Robert Chasemore. Even about that she'd been distinctly dubious. In fact, though, they'd gone on from there, she and Andrew. Now, they often had meals together after work, and they shared what was undoubtedly a friendship. With regular meetings, cups of coffee, working lunches, and finally, last week, one evening at an expensive restaurant. So she and Andrew *were* progressing, however slowly. The question was, where to?

Very likely, of course, she was simply his equivalent to Leo's Sister Henderson. An easy-going friendship between colleagues, pleasant and useful, that could endure for years, and would never be anything else.

After all, at the Central they said not only had Andrew taken a hard knock over Gillian, but he was still in love with her. Naturally, in that case, he wasn't going to offer love or marriage to anyone else. Only companionship.

She should be very happy with such an outcome, Nicola informed herself firmly. She had so much more than she'd have dared to hope five years ago. She ought to try to be satisfied with what she had, instead of crying for the sun, the moon and the stars.

The trouble was, though, even their companionship would soon be over and gone. Her post as Robert Chasemore's registrar came to an end in the autumn, and she'd leave the general theatre. Unless she did something about it fast, that would be the end of seeing Andrew—other than from a seat in the gallery when Robert Chasemore happened to be giving a tricky gas, that it was her duty to watch.

CHAPTER TWO

The Secret Garden

A WEEK LATER Andrew invited Nicola again for a meal at
the Country Garden.

One thing was sure. She wasn't going to wear the
Liberty silk. In her lunch hour she rushed off to the little
boutique in Great St Anne's, Francesca's, to search for
some gear with sex appeal.

Her first choice was a dramatic cerise linen. In it she
would be fashionable, poised, self-assured—exactly
how she never felt with Andrew.

Francesca, though, the boutique owner—a slim
blonde in her thirties, who genuinely loved clothes and
dressing people stunningly—pressed sapphire blue
muslin separates on her. 'Do try them on,' she urged.
'The colour is perfect for you.'

Nicola tried them on, and bought them—not so much
for the colour as for the cleavage, the bare midriff below
the knotted top, and the figure-hugging skirt.

Andrew's eyes were riveted.

He'd never looked at her like that before. So that was
one question answered, she told herself ecstatically. He
wasn't physically immune to her. It must have been
simply that in the past it had never crossed his mind to
regard her as a sex object. Right. She was going to
change that. From now on she was going to throw her
sexuality at him. Daily. Nightly, if she had the opportunity. To hell with Gillian and the past. There'd be no
more standing about, wondering if he was going to
notice her. What was more, she'd stop, stat, treating him
so much like the eminent senior he undoubtedly was.
She'd be casual, of course, if it killed her. But on-
coming. Always on-coming.

'Care for a coffee in my place?' she asked a bemused Andrew, given the full treatment throughout the evening. Her voice was low and seductive, her blue eyes proffered an invitation that was unmistakable, and he could see right down her cleavage.

To his own astonishment he managed to refuse. Afterwards he wondered how on earth he'd pulled it off—and why? What was supposed to be so sacred about Nicola Lancaster? If any other girl had behaved like that, he'd never have rushed off in the opposite direction. So why was Nicola different?

Alone in her flat, Nicola was vibrating with joy. Not a doubt of it, he'd been longing to accept her offer. He'd had a struggle to say no.

So now she knew. He was interested in her as a female. He needed no more than a bit of encouragement, and from now on she was going to see he received it. Andrew, she informed her bedroom wall, Andrew, my beloved, I'm coming to get you. Never mind love or marriage, I'll have whatever you're offering.

During the following week, in her free moments she planned a new wardrobe of sizzling garments to wow Andrew, totally unaware that as she was, bundled up in a theatre gown, her hair screwed back under its cap, she had only to cast him a liquid blue glance and he was ready to pick her up bodily and fling himself on top of her, the patient abandoned on the table.

He was short-tempered, cross and snappy in the theatre all week. The only method he could find of maintaining any sort of concentration, with that blue-eyed bombshell smouldering away at the patient's head.

Sister Jarvis was on to it at once.

'It's Dr Lancaster,' she explained to her staff nurse. 'He's finally gone overboard for her, and he doesn't know what to do with himself.'

The staff nurse made a crude suggestion.

'Yes, well, of course,' Stella Jarvis agreed tranquilly—

she was a tranquil personality, one of the reasons she made a good theatre sister. 'But hardly in the middle of surgery, dear. Hence the temper.'

Instead of the Country Garden, that week, he took Nicola to the theatre, and supper afterwards—at the Dorchester, which shattered her. They ate smoked salmon followed by fillet steak, and then a mouthwatering dessert of fresh raspberries and peaches smothered in cream loaded with brandy. They had a different wine with each course—and the entire meal was wasted. Enchanted with one another, they tasted nothing.

Nicola, who'd had no opportunity to go further afield, had been back to the boutique in Great St Anne's. In no way was she going out two weeks running with Andrew wearing the blue muslin, effective though it had undoubtedly proved.

This time round, she chose a very different dress, a mere scrap of black silk with that season's low back and a slim skirt that shifted with every breath she took. Francesca was enthusiastic. 'It's perfect on you. And you can wear it *anywhere*.' Neither of them, at that moment, envisaged the Dorchester. 'No one will remember it if you just ring the changes with accessories.' She was well aware of the demands of a busy hospital—nearly all her customers rushed in at the last minute from the Central, with hardly a moment or a penny to spare. 'Different beads, and stockings to match them, and you're away,' she said.

'Beads? Stockings?' Nicola was vague, lost in an attempt to forecast Andrew's reaction.

'Black strappy sandals.' Francesca was lost in her own vision, a picture of this astounding girl dressed up and out on the town in *her* frock. 'And a black bag. You've got those?'

Nicola nodded dreamily. 'Yes, I can manage that.'

'Then, say, jade green beads and stockings?'

Nicola looked dubious.

'Or cinnamon, then, for a quieter, more expensive look. But you must have matching stockings. Or if you want to be truly up-market, how about a simple rope of pearls and black stockings with clocks?'

'I don't run to pearls, I'm afraid.'

'Good grief, girl, they don't have to be *real*.'

Nicola couldn't see herself going out with Andrew wearing a huge rope of fake pearls, so she bought the cinnamon beads and the stockings to match.

Andrew couldn't take his eyes off her. Because of the theatre, he'd left the Porsche at the hospital, and they'd used taxis. When they drew up outside Nicola's block in St Anne's Square, she extended her invitation. 'Coming up? A coffee?'

He gave a sort of groan, and remarked, in a grinding and off-putting voice that would once have devastated her, 'Oh God, Nicola, it's a mistake, you know. The last thing I ought—*all right*.'

He paid off the taxi—the driver winked meaningfully, but Andrew ignored this and promptly cut down on the tip, too—and followed her up the steps and into the lift.

Nicola found her keys, unlocked the door, stepped inside, and melted into his arms. There was no escape. Andrew couldn't jostle past her in the narrow passage, he hadn't even room to open the front door again behind him and rush like an idiot out into the square. Not that he wanted to do anything of the sort. He'd been longing to take her into his arms all evening. All week. All year. For ever.

It was a mistake, though. He shouldn't be doing it. It was great. And he was going to go on doing it, now he'd begun.

'God, Nicola, you're so lovely. You feel as marvellous as I knew you would.' He devoured her a second time, and at last came up for air to say almost accusingly 'If you *knew* how long I've wanted to do this.'

'Why ever didn't you, then?'

'Oh, love'—

He'd never called her that before.

—'because I—you—you're so much younger, for one thing. You haven't been married as I have, and—and—'

'All right, so I've never been married. But I fail to see what that has to do with here and now.'

'Not with here and now, perhaps,' he agreed. He kissed her again, less passionately, more, she realised delightedly, more lovingly.

She'd moved into a state of tranquil bliss. What came next, or tomorrow, or next week, meant nothing. Here and now was all she needed. She was held in Andrew's arms, against his thudding heart—not a doubt of that, either, his heart was thudding. He was excited, too. Let him just try to pretend he wasn't.

Nicola herself was both excited and curiously at peace. More at peace than she'd ever been. She'd come home, to a safe haven for ever.

It was precisely this reaction that had been worrying Giles.

It worried Andrew, too. 'Nicola,' he was saying softly, smoothing the cloud of dark hair from her brow with tender adoring fingers.

To be touched like this by Andrew was all her dreams come true, and she shut her eyes and basked in the delight. 'M-mm?' she murmured, hoping that he was about to suggest making love there and then, exactly where they were, in her minute little hall.

'This simply isn't fair to you, you know.'

She opened her eyes. 'Why not?' This was the point where he was going to tell her he didn't love her. He still loved Gillian, and that was what he was going to say, because he was one of the most honest men Nicola had ever known. She braced herself to hear it, finding it already more unbearable than she'd ever imagined it could be.

'Because I've no intention of marrying again,' he said baldly.

Not quite what she'd expected, of course, but near enough, and probably merely a kinder way of putting it. 'So what?' she asked. 'Was anyone talking about marriage? If so, it wasn't me.' She put her lips to his again, explored his mouth. Never in her life had she taken the initiative like this, but how should he know? He had to think her sophisticated, knowledgeable, practised in love. Only then would he overcome these inconvenient principles of his—about which Giles had been so clear, and so extraordinarily accurate.

Andrew kissed her back hard, his mouth demanding, urgent. So, she could feel, was the rest of his body. Take me, take me and make love to me, she wanted to shout.

Sadly, though, she wasn't that sort of girl, it appeared. Her head could plan it, but her lips refused to form the words. All that actually came out was a muted little murmur of 'I love you.'

He heard it, and it was the wrong thing to have said.

He drew back. 'Oh God, Nicola, you don't, do you?'

Hastily she summoned the sophistication she'd intended to display. 'At this particular moment I certainly do,' she told him, in tones she was determined to make throaty and voluptuous. 'Tomorrow, next week—that remains to be seen, wouldn't you say?'

'Nicola.' He sighed heavily. 'You'll be the undoing of me.'

At that she had quite genuinely chuckled. 'That was the general idea,' she agreed cheerfully. 'So what are we waiting for?'

He gave in. What man wouldn't? Even so, he'd felt compelled to utter a final warning. 'As long as you understand.'

'What am I supposed to understand?' Not that she didn't know perfectly well what he meant. As long as you understand that I don't love you. That it's not like

Gillian, and never will be. That's what he was trying to tell her. And that was the price she had to pay, she'd known it all along.

'That it—we—that it's strictly a temporary affair,' he said, hating himself. 'Not in any way permanent.'

'Of course not.' She was airy. 'Here today, gone tomorrow.' She kissed her hand to him. 'So, I repeat, what are we waiting for?'

That was the first time they made love. But not the last, not by any means. And from that evening onwards Nicola walked the hospital in her own cloud of glory, untouchable by fate or disaster. She was radiant. Suddenly it had all happened. She had Andrew. All right, so she didn't have the love he'd given Gillian, but what she did have was wonderful. In a daze of delight she trod the pavements between Andrew's maisonette in Harley Street and the Central, between the hospital and her own small flat in St Anne's Square.

Andrew was happy too. Much happier than he'd expected to be, though a little worried still. But their relationship was so obviously what they both wanted and needed—why have second thoughts, or worry about Nicola? She was independent, with her own career, and no one could expect her to cut herself off from sexual experience until the day she decided to marry.

Even so, for her sake more than his own, he was careful. They could say what they liked about him, but he wasn't having them laying their lecherous tongues to Nicola. Everyone in general surgery might guess at once what had happened—he was right there—but no one should have so much as a glimpse of the where and when.

He was over-optimistic. No one in the general theatre needed Stella Jarvis any longer to notify them what was going on. They could see it for themselves.

Down at Halchester, Giles heard more than enough. He rang Nicola up at her flat in the evening, caught her at home, and alone—he was careful to enquire if anyone was with her before he opened his onslaught. 'What the hell is all this about you and Andrew, anyway?'

'Andrew and I are going out together, as you've evidently heard.' She was short. 'So you were wrong, weren't you, about one meal at the Country Garden not meaning anything?'

'I just hope you know what you're up to, that's all.'

Exactly the attitude he'd adopted when he'd warned her off Andrew at lunch in Giovanni's, and she'd had more than enough of it, useful though it had undoubtedly been in the first place. 'Of course I do,' she said curtly, and put the telephone down.

She wished she actually felt as confident. Inwardly, she was beginning to be terrified. Because now she had what she'd wanted for so long, she couldn't face losing it. Yet one day she and Andrew would separate, move on, away—and how she'd survive she couldn't imagine.

Stupid to panic. Here and now they were together, they were in love, happiness surrounded them both. No need to peer anxiously into the future. Today was what counted, and today was wonderful.

The days stretched out and made weeks, weeks and then months of a hot summer that was the answer to all Nicola's dreams.

On a Friday in late July, she went over to the hospital with even more bounce than usual. She and Andrew were both off for the weekend. Emergencies apart, they'd have Friday night, Saturday and Sunday together. Except that Giles would be in London, and she supposed she ought to spare an hour or two for him, tiresome as he'd been recently. But lunch on Saturday would be enough, surely? He'd be busy himself, in any case—he was coming up from the accident unit at Halchester, either on Friday night or Saturday morning, according to when he could get off, for a weekend course with lectures and operations in various London hospitals. The course would open that afternoon at the Central, when Andrew would be the demonstrating surgeon, the list consisting of what was known in the department as 'cold' surgery—in other words, the cases were not emergencies, but accident victims who'd been admitted earlier as casualties, and who were now ready for detailed surgical repair to improve the function of injured limbs. Nicola would be in the theatre with Andrew throughout the afternoon—Robert Chasemore had made her responsible for the anaesthetics throughout the list.

When she arrived at 1.45 p.m. to see to the first patient, the gallery was already filling up, with young accident surgeons from all over the country pouring in.

The list went smoothly, and by four o'clock they were on to the final patient, a motor cyclist admitted as an emergency a month earlier, too shocked to stand more than the minimum of action needed to save his life. He was strong enough now, though, for his damaged body to be repaired in this long session on the operating table.

Giles arrived just as this final surgery was starting, and from a late-comer's position at the back of the gallery he looked down into the brilliantly lit capsule of green-robed activity below. Although he'd come especially to watch his former chief, he found he was scarcely conscious of Andrew's tall form and busy hands, mesmerised instead by Nicola, her slight and elegant figure misleadingly bulky in her theatre gown, as she sat perched on a stool by the patient's head, observing the patient, twiddling the knobs on the gas and air mixture. For years they had had this easy-going friendship, he reminded himself. So why had she all at once acquired this fascination for him?

The answer made him despair of his own common-sense. Only since she had taken up with Andrew had he himself felt like this about her. As soon, that is, as she was unattainable.

Andrew began stitching up, the gallery emptied. Giles, though, was in no hurry. Nicola would go through to the recovery room, and wouldn't emerge until she was satisfied with the patient's progress. So he had time in hand. Time to pull himself together before he met her.

As she came through the automatic doors and out on to the landing outside the general theatre suites, she saw him waiting, gave him a smile that, to his rage, made his heart turn over. 'Giles—great to see you. I thought you weren't going to be able to get away in time for this afternoon's list?'

'I caught the train by a split second. But here I am, so how about a boozy night on the town? Perhaps take in a disco. I want to live it up a bit while I've got the chance.'

Her blue eyes evaded his. 'Giles, I'm so sorry, but I really can't. Not tonight. How about lunch tomorrow? That any good?'

'Have to be, I suppose.' He might have known it. 'Andrew, I suppose. That's still on, is it?' He'd honestly thought that affair might be over by now, have ended as abruptly—not to mention crazily—as it had begun.

Nicola was thoroughly irritated with him. If he was going to start arguing again about Andrew, she was thankful she hadn't made time to go out with him that evening. Lunch tomorrow would be more than enough. What was more, she had no intention of standing about by the lifts, on the receiving end of another of his lectures about how she should run her life. 'Look,' she said. 'I must rush. Sorry. One o'clock at Giovanni's tomorrow?'

He was sulky. 'I suppose I'll have to make do with that. All the same—'

'See you then.' Nicola stepped into a convenient lift as the doors were closing, and was wafted downwards, leaving him seething. She came out into a shining summer evening, and began walking across to Harley Street.

Andrew lived at the top of one of those tall London terrace houses put up in the eighteenth century, and beautiful and functional still. He'd acquired the lease from one of the heart surgeons who, on his retirement, had gone to live permanently in his country cottage. Nicola had first been there for Andrew's housewarming party, and from the moment she'd set foot inside the charming attic sitting room and library on the top floor— the bedrooms were one floor down—she'd been enchanted. Since then she'd often been, in a group from the hospital for drinks, say, to meet overseas visitors, or with Robert Chasemore, to work out, with Andrew, his houseman and registrar, the details of the following day's list, or that week's admissions and discharges. She always enjoyed being there.

It was wonderful to arrive knowing he'd be alone and waiting for her.

On this sultry summer evening she found him in the roof garden. The heart surgeon, always a country lover, who gardened ferociously in his limited spare time, had had the roof strengthened so that he could indulge his hobby in the heart of the city. Andrew had taken over where he left off, and the little garden had become, for those lucky enough to be invited into it, one of the Central's favourite summer haunts.

One of the alterations Andrew had made had been to put up fencing. Hopelessly windy up there, he'd said. Like riding out a gale in the open channel. He'd installed six-foot-high wattle fencing, and at once the garden, until then a charming urban folly preening itself with urns and furniture among the chimney pots, was transformed into a country retreat. For most of the summer months he slept out there, and recently he'd made secret hidden love there to Nicola.

When she arrived he was stretched out in one of the long chairs, wearing—unlike her, in her working denim, he'd had time to change, she saw enviously—white jeans and a navy shirt. As she came through the French windows, she caught the scent of the jasmine that climbed everywhere. Andrew shot out of his chair, took her in his arms, and they kissed with the wild excitement that continued to astonish them both.

It was Andrew who broke away. It usually was. He regarded her clinically. 'Worn out,' he informed her, not entirely to her delight. 'You need a drink.' He moved across to the teak table, mixed her something in one of his heavy smoked glass tumblers. Ice clinked encouragingly as he brought it to her. 'Lie back with that and relax. Soak up the last of the sun. You could do with it, you know. You look pale.'

While it was marvellous to be cherished, most of all by Andrew, Nicola could have done without the final remark.

'I thought we might stay in and eat,' he added. 'All right?'

She sipped the cold delicious drink. 'Very much all right. I don't at the moment care if I never move again.' Emptying her mind of the problems of the day, basking not so much in the last of the sun as in the joy of being with him again, she collapsed into one of the long chairs and closed her eyes.

Andrew watched her. Slight, lovely—and so vulnerable, he reminded himself. The thought of what he might be able to do to her inadvertently, of how easily he could hurt her, was beginning to frighten him. And he didn't know how to deal with the problem. Too late, now, to stop what they'd started. He'd not been prepared for the force of their loving. He'd never expected her to house, in that slight frame, so much passion. A passion, it had to be said, to match his own.

This evening, though, she was exhausted. He could see that at a glance. And it was hardly surprising. The end of a hard week. And London had experienced one of its rare heatwaves.

Standing over her as she lay back in the chair, he smoothed her high brow with gentle fingers, and as the minutes passed, he watched anxiety and tension dissipate, and her face take on the softer and so much younger look that he had already learned to treasure. She was infinitely precious to him.

'How soon would you like to eat?'

Her thoughts neither on food nor drink, she wanted only to enjoy the bliss of being quietly alone with him at last. 'Whenever you like.'

'We could have our meal out here.'

'Terrific. Shall I—'

'You stay put. I'll fetch the food. All ready, in any case.'

He brought smoked trout, wedges of lemon, a mound of wholemeal bread, butter in his pottery dish, and a bottle of Hock in an ice bucket.

Nicola sat up smartly, attacked the meal with zest.

Andrew smiled at her. 'One of the things I like about you is your unflagging appetite.'

'One of the things I like about you,' she retorted—to be able to cheek Andrew mildly was exhilarating—'is your marvellous food. And your super garden. That's what I come for, of course.' She smiled at him joyfully.

Between them, they cleared the trout, and the wholemeal bread, and Andrew poured more Hock.

'Delicious,' she told him. 'I must say, I feel altogether different now.' She stretched luxuriously.

He was lost. Out of his chair, bending over her, he took her face between his two hands, and kissed her slowly and long. 'Out here, under the sky?' he murmured finally. 'Would you like that, love?'

'You know I would,' she told him, and folded loving arms round his broad shoulders and held him to her.

As they clung together through the long summer evening Nicola prayed inwardly. If only it need never end, if only life could always be like this, herself and

Andrew, alone in their secret garden, for ever loving under a summer sky. She was far too much ashamed of this to mention it—it was a foolish adolescent longing that she must hide, keep to her amazingly foolish adolescent self.

The late summer dusk had come down when she awoke to hear Andrew saying something. She muttered drowsily, turned in his arms.

'Strawberries,' he said. 'There were meant to be strawberries for supper. I forgot them.' He kissed her silky shoulder.

She smoothed his hair, felt the line of his brow, touched with the tips of her fingers the lips she loved so desperately. An ache of love ran through her, and she arched in his arms.

At once his hands held her, and his nails dug into her flesh.

She laughed, drew her own nails down his spine, and they were locked together in another loving until, again, they lay in drowsy peace.

'Those strawberries,' he announced in the darkness. 'I'll get them.' He was up, striding into the house, to reappear with a candle flickering in a balloon glass. He set it down beside her. 'Look after that, while I fetch the strawberries.'

He returned with a bowl of strawberries and a jug of cream, poured the last of the wine, and they sat together eating and drinking in the candlelit night, until at last, reluctantly, in the early hours of the morning, they slipped indoors, showered and dressed, and Andrew walked Nicola home to her own flat.

Outside her own front door he kissed her again. 'Thank you, love, for a memorable evening.' To her surprise, he added, with a chuckle, 'And to think that there I was, before you arrived, waiting for the telephone to ring, and it would be you, saying you couldn't make it.'

'Ring and—?' She stared at him. 'Why on earth did you imagine—'

'Giles Yorke is up, isn't he? He was hanging about on the landing, waiting for you, I thought, and I felt sure you'd be spending the evening with him.'

'Oh well, he did suggest it. But I said I couldn't. So I'm having lunch with him tomorrow.'

CHAPTER THREE

A New Post?

NICOLA was looking forward to hearing Giles' news—about his job at St Mark's, about his catamaran, that he sailed enthusiastically in every spare minute. Skilfully, too—last year he'd come third in the national championships. As long as he kept off the subject of herself and Andrew, she knew she'd enjoy lunch with him.

She was out of luck. Giles, too, had thought out his approach with a good deal of care. He was genuinely worried about Nicola. Leaving aside his own feelings about her, what was going to happen to her when Andrew, as he undoubtedly would, dropped her for some new and sexier partner?

Privately, Giles was astonished that the affair had even begun. If he'd been at the Central still, instead of down at St Mark's, a hundred miles away, he'd have made sure it had never so much as got off the ground. He had to recognise, though, that trying to warn Nicola about the disaster he could see approaching would get him nowhere, and he'd thought up an alternative plan.

His aim was simple. To separate her from Andrew, and the sooner the better.

As soon as they were seated in Giovanni's, he began enquiring as anxiously as he knew how about her next post. He was a slick operator, and he'd chosen his ground well.

Like every other registrar, Nicola spent a fair amount of her limited free time brooding over her career prospects and her next job. She had only a few months to go in her present post. After that, what? She was hoping for a senior registrar's post in London, but so far she hadn't managed to get one. One particular vacancy at the

Central everyone assured her she had a good chance to land, but when the time came a friend of hers, a year senior, who had notched up the same posts and the same qualifications, but who had spent an extra year as a resident at the Mayo Clinic in the USA, had landed the job. Nicola had soldiered on, putting in for other posts all over London and the home counties. She had been shortlisted for nearly all of them, and grew accustomed to attending interviews. Unfortunately what she also grew accustomed to was failing to be appointed to the post. Beaten, in every case, by a man, too.

She set her teeth and went on trying. No use moaning about unfairness. This was how it was, and she had to live with it.

Giles agreed with her about this. Where they began arguing was over her only alternative plan. This was, if she hadn't succeeded in obtaining a senior registrar's post by October, when her present job came to an end, to stand in for a year in the orthopaedic intensive care unit at the Central. The registrar there had won a fellowship to the Johns Hopkins, the famous American hospital.

'You can't do that,' Giles exploded. This was just what he had been afraid of. That she'd take stop-gap jobs in the Central, simply for the sake of staying with Andrew, who'd drop her like yesterday's evening paper the moment some new sexy house physician swam into his orbit. Giles himself had always been under the impression that Nicola was not a very sexy girl. Brainy, and all that. A poppet. But sexy, no. 'Once you start taking on jobs like that you're doomed,' he told her angrily.

Nicola raised quizzical dark brows above coolly interrogative blue eyes glinting coldly, a trick she had perfected to deal with students on ward rounds who tried to trip her up. 'Doomed?' she repeated, making the word sound ridiculous and melodramatic.

Giles refused to give in. 'I mean it. Doomed. The day you take up any stop-gap job like that, leading nowhere, you'll be throwing your future down the drain. You'll simply spend the rest of your life standing in for people who go sick, or win fellowships, or drop dead. You'll never get a senior post, you'll be the odd-job girl around the Central. A permanent dogsbody, with a brilliant future behind you.'

There was a lot of truth in this, and Nicola knew it. She tried to be reasonable. 'What do you suggest, then? I need a post in October, and so far that's the only one I've actually been offered. Facts are facts.'

'Ah, but have you tried?'

'Of course I've tried.' She could have screamed at him. 'Listen, I've been telling you.' She flexed long narrow fingers, began telling off the posts she'd applied for.

He interrupted her. 'I know. I heard. You listen, duckie. They were all near London. Right?' He was accusing.

'Well, yes, but—'

'That's the whole point. You aren't really trying. You're waiting to have it handed to you on a plate. You haven't put in for a single job more than half an hour from the Central. All you're really thinking about is hanging round Andrew.' He glared at her. 'Nicky, you simply can't go on like this. Not unless you're ready to throw your career away for ever while you dance attendance on Andrew like some besotted groupie.'

This left Nicola momentarily speechless.

Giles did some more glaring, and then shrugged. 'I'm surprised, frankly, that Andrew allows you to do it. He must know as well as I do what it's going to cost you.'

Nicola drank her by now tepid coffee and looked distant. She was not going to get into any sort of argument with Giles about what Andrew ought or ought not to do. Discussing her career and prospects was one thing. Discussing Andrew was out.

Giles read her closed expression, and returned hurriedly to the subject of her career. 'Have you, for instance, put in for a single post more than twenty miles from Piccadilly?

'Actually, I suppose—'

'You haven't. Look, Nicky, at least promise me this. If a suitable post is advertised, you'll put in for it—convincingly, too. With good references and nice pristine copies of your *curriculum vitae*.'

She was injured. 'I would anyway.'

'Fine. And now I must scarper. I have to cross London—I'm due at the Hammersmith operating theatre in less than half an hour. See you, sweetie. And remember what I said.'

'I'll think about it.' And she did, far too much for comfort. She didn't like his arguments, but he could be right, she had to admit. What he didn't understand was that none of it mattered. Loving Andrew was more important than her next post.

What was more, Giles' opinion was based on a mis-reading of her character. She wasn't, as he insisted on assuming, vulnerable. If she was the frail plant he appeared to imagine, she'd never have been able to complete her training. Many times, then, she'd been certain she'd bitten off more than she could chew. The first occasion she'd been actually in the theatre, and a patient was opened up on the table, she'd thought she was going to disgrace herself and pass out flat on the floor. She hadn't at all been able to take in what was going on, and she would have been incapable of assist-ing, had anyone been so demented as to ask her. No one, of course, did. But that evening, thinking it over, she'd fallen into the depths of depression. Her dreams of surgery were finished, over. But she'd come through that, found she enjoyed theatre work, and a year later,

when Andrew had to break it to her that she was the
wrong build for a surgeon, she'd been shocked. And
back in the depths of depression.

This was how life had to be. Up and down, Striving
and struggling, and being afraid you'd failed. But
bashing on, and then discovering you'd made it, after all.

Loving Andrew was much the same. Somehow, without knowing how it had come about, a secret dream had
turned into reality. Daily life. And whatever happened
in the end, at least she would have had this. The most
important thing there could be in anyone's life, a love
that swept her off her feet, that made demands on her,
that brought out feelings she hadn't known she possessed. She might not be able to see how, when it
ended, she'd survive. But somehow she would. Because
by then she'd be a different person, she'd have grown
and developed, exactly as she had in the years between
first-year student and qualified doctor. What was more,
of one thing she was certain. Every day, every second, of
loving Andrew would have been worthwhile.

So was she going to ignore what Giles said? Take the
one-year post in orthopaedic intensive care?

Somehow this plan upset her. It seemed too feeble a
surrender. She'd be giving up all she believed in, like
independence, responsibility for her own future. She'd
be giving up, Giles had been right there, her career in
medicine. She thought, still, she had it in her to be
first-rate. Maybe she hadn't, she wouldn't be the first to
discover she'd over-estimated her own abilities. But if
she gave up trying for senior registrar posts she'd have
thrown her career away without ever finding out. She'd
be that old stereotype, a girl hopelessly in love who
allowed everything else in life to pass her by. The world
well lost for love.

Why not? That was what she wanted, wasn't it?

No, it wasn't. She wanted to play her part in the world,
not retire into a harem.

If she was a man she wouldn't be so daft. She'd put in for every job there was, no matter whom she loved or where they happened to be.

This thought upset her more than anything else. To see herself suddenly as an emotional girl, behaving quite differently in a given situation from her male colleagues—this really threw her.

Arguing with herself as she walked from intensive care to the wards, from the wards to her office, from her office to the operating theatre, she battled through a week of swinging moods and changing decisions. One evening she would be certain she'd reached a conclusion. Blow her career. She was staying with Andrew.

The next morning she'd have second thoughts. What was she thinking of doing? Throwing her future in medicine away.

Her only peace came when she was with Andrew. She knew then that parting was unthinkable. No price was too high to pay.

Then Andrew himself took a hand. 'By the way,' he said. 'I've been meaning to ask you. How did the lunch with Giles go? Satisfactory?'

It was a wet evening—the heat wave had broken in thunderstorms—and they were sitting in his attic living room drinking coffee.

'Not really.' She shrugged. 'A bit tiresome, in fact.'

'Tiresome?' She'd surprised him. Whatever he'd expected her lunch with Giles to have been—and she would have been astonished to know how much time he'd spent wondering about it—it wasn't this.

'Yes, it was rather.' Too late, she wished she hadn't spoken.

'What was he tiresome about?' Andrew thought he was on to something. What was Giles up to? Andrew had always suspected him. Nicola's oldest friend, he breathed down her neck and told her how to run her life. What had he been putting her up to now?

'As I haven't managed to get a senior registrar's post yet, he thinks I ought to be putting in for posts outside London, not settling for the one-year job in the orthopaedic department.' The words came unwillingly. Nicola knew what was going to happen, she could see it coming with the inevitability of the Severn bore. It was going to sweep her up and deposit her somewhere else. Why on earth had she been such a fool as to let Andrew find out?

And here it came. 'He's absolutely right, of course,' Andrew told her. 'So you should.' He was ashamed of himself. He ought to have been thinking about Nicola's career, not Giles. That he hadn't done so had been selfish, if not negligent. Nicola had once been one of his students, she remained ten years his junior, and he'd done nothing, nothing at all, to see that she found a post suited to her exceptional abilities. What had stopped him? His need of her. He'd put satisfying what the Victorians would have called his lust ahead of her personal future. Self-indulgent egotist. From now on he must put Nicola's career ahead of everything. 'Have you checked the journals this week?' he demanded crisply. 'Any openings?'

'I—I haven't looked. Not so far.'

Andrew reached for the *British Medical Journal*, lying there conveniently on his coffee table, flicked through to the end pages where the advertisements were. 'Um— let's see. Anaesthetics, here we are. Consultant, in the midlands. Senior registrar. Ah ha. It's at Southampton. Good place. University, too. You'd better put straight in.'

'I suppose so,' Nicola agreed bleakly.

Giles and Andrew had decided for her. So much for her worry-gutting. They'd taken over, without hesitation, and independently reached the same conclusion. They had to be right.

She wrote to Southampton, and also to Inverness,

where a job came up the following week. She also wrote
to a hospital in Bristol, where the consultant had been a
student with Andrew. Andrew, it appeared, had been
asking around, and was putting himself out in order to
find her a suitable post in October.

Many people, she knew, would have considered that
to have Andrew Ritchie hunting for a job for them was
an achievement in its own right. A few years back she
would have thought so herself.

She was short-listed for Southampton and Bristol, but
not, to her immense relief, for Inverness.

'Up in the highlands,' Andrew said unfairly, 'they
probably don't know there are any women doctors.'

'The trouble is,' Nicola pointed out—but whatever
she might pretend, was she sorry? Or was she beginning
to be glad?—'In Bristol and Southampton they may
know all about them, but still not want one.'

'You must just keep on trying. None of it's anything to
do with your own ability, it's simply the chauvinists in
charge. To be on the safe side, I'll ask around a bit.'

At Southampton they chose one of their own registrars, and it was obvious that this was what they'd
intended to do from the beginning. Advertising had
been no more than a formality.

In Bristol they called her back for a second interview—there was a woman on the board—and she
thought she had a good chance. But then they called two
others back as well, and at the end of the day chose one
of them.

'He was very good,' she told Andrew. 'He had more
experience than I have—he'd had a senior registrar's
post already. But none of his posts had been at teaching
hospitals, so I had the edge over him there. However, he
had the edge over me by being male, so there it is.'

'Thank God you aren't male,' Andrew said. 'There
are some advantages, I hope you're prepared to admit.'

'I'm prepared to admit,' Nicola agreed into his chest.

She took a deep breath, and forgot about the jobs.

The next day, though, she spoke severely to herself. She mustn't simply stand about hoping that nothing would come of all this writing off and being interviewed. Hoping that she'd be able to slip quietly into the post in the orthopaedic department because, although she'd done her best, no job had come up for her.

She couldn't stick around for ever at the Central, still be there when the day came, as it inevitably would, when Andrew began to lose interest in her, when he wanted out. To go a little too soon would be far better than to go too late. To stay and watch him fall for someone else, or even, as some people believed would happen, be reunited with Gillian when she completed her contract in Saudi Arabia—never.

Giles was right. She must grit her teeth, go ahead and leave.

As she might have guessed, Giles himself came up with the solution. He found a post for her at St Mark's. Ever since their lunch he must have been working away, winning friends and influencing people on her behalf. Now he rang her and told her to put in for a post as senior registrar of the intensive care unit attached to the accident and emergency department. She did as he said, and only a fortnight later was called for interview. They offered her the post.

At last she had landed a senior registrar's post—at a good hospital, too. To see herself moving up the promotion ladder she'd so often despaired of climbing induced a sense of real triumph. Elated, she couldn't help looking forward to the job itself, to the opportunities for increasing responsibility.

And the post was in intensive care, a department she'd always loved, though some of her friends were unable to understand this. They would have disliked, they told her, never dealing with patients other than the dangerously ill, who, the moment they were at all improved, moved away to a ward, to someone else's care. There was seldom a chance to know them as people. Nicola, though, found this more than compensated for by her awareness that it was her job to keep her patients alive, to improve them despite the odds stacked against them, to give them back a future, in fact, so that they could go off to the wards and make normal progress, finally to return home. This made every day's work worthwhile.

Each day was a struggle, of course, and you couldn't win them all. In intensive care they lost more patients than in other departments. But though this upset her when it happened, in some ways it stimulated her to further effort, made her search for ways of keeping people alive through the critical phase of their illness. Today, in intensive care in the Central, they were able to save patients who wouldn't even, say ten years earlier, have been admitted. They would have died in the ambulance. Progress was made daily. And she was part of it. Her thought, her decisions, her skill and her care were keeping patients alive who might otherwise have died.

Down at St Mark's, if she accepted this new post, she'd be, under the consultant, in overall charge of the intensive care unit attached to the accident department. The hourly, day-to-day responsibility would be mainly hers. Until now this had never been the case, and the prospect of it exhilarated her. One day, perhaps, some discovery of hers, some method she used to treat these dangerously ill patients, would lead to another advance in therapeutics. She'd save, not only the patient there in the bed under her care, but others she'd never meet, patients in units up and down the country, who'd benefit from an advance she'd made.

This was what made the long hours and the hard work, the broken nights and the interrupted meals, not only worthwhile, but hopeful and exciting. This was why she valued her job, why she couldn't imagine life without it.

If only, though, the new post had been just a little

nearer London, instead of down on the coast a hundred miles away. If only it didn't involve this separation from Andrew. She had to hesitate. Was she right to take the job? Would it in the end be better to turn it down, wait until she found a post nearer London? In the meantime she could have this extra year at the Central—it was not too late to say she'd like the orthopaedic post. Another year shared with Andrew.

Giles, apparently, was able to read her mind. He rang her, demanding to know if she'd written off yet accepting the St Mark's post. Caught out, she'd hedged.

'Nicky, pull yourself together. Wake up. This is your last chance.' He was maddened, she could hear it in his voice. 'If you don't break free now, when the right post is there waiting for you, you never will. Show a bit of independence for once. Follow your own star, not Andrew Ritchie's. If you let this opportunity slip, you're finished.'

She knew he had to be right. All the same, she didn't write off to St Mark's. She couldn't quite bring herself to do that, to make the break from London and the Central inevitable. She was ashamed of her own feebleness, and yet—yet—she shook her head. She couldn't do it.

It was Andrew, though he didn't know it, who made up her mind for her. Catching her up at the door of the recovery room, straight from the theatre, in his blood-drenched gown, his mask hanging, he spoke abruptly. 'Nicola. A word. This evening. I'm sorry, but we'll have to call it off.'

It was his birthday, and they'd been going to celebrate. Her face fell.

'Have to be another evening instead.' He was curt. That he was hating every second of this, hating himself most of all, didn't occur to Nicola. 'Thing is, I can't imagine why, but Gillian—er—' unusually for him, he floundered '—my—um—my former wife, I don't think actually you ever knew her.' He paused.

Nicola said nothing.

'She rang this morning at breakfast. She's here in London for a couple of days, and she wanted me to meet her for a meal this evening. So I had to say yes.' Another pause.

Nicola broke it. 'Of course you must meet her,' she assured him, in the bright encouraging tones a good nanny might have used. No one, least of all Andrew, should have so much as a glimpse of the desolation that had invaded her. Her world lay in ruins, but no one must be allowed to know. Not at any price.

'She flies back to Saudi Arabia tomorrow.' Andrew had not been taken in by Nicola's false brightness. Gillian's sudden appearance in his life had shaken her to the core, and his remark was meant to reassure both of them. Tomorrow, he meant, Gillian would fly back to her own hospital three thousand miles away, and they'd be free of her again. Whatever it was she wanted would be known, and, he hoped a little desperately, settled. Finished with. What the hell did she want, anyway? 'I'll take her to Giovanni's for a quick bite, and then tomorrow evening we can have the dinner we planned,' he added, his eyes searching Nicola's.

She turned her head away. 'Yes, of course,' she said with the same false brightness. 'See you tomorrow, then. Now I really must get on.' She walked into the recovery room, and began talking very fast to the staff nurse.

In her lunch hour she took a sandwich and a cup of coffee to her office, shut the door, sat down at her desk and wrote off to St Mark's accepting the post.

Acutely miserable, she sat back in her chair. There, that was done. And not before time. She ought to have accepted by return of post. Well, better late than never. Giles, at least, would be pleased.

She'd ring him. After all, he'd found the job for her, she ought to let him know she'd at last got round to accepting it. And it would be nice, reassuring, to hear his voice when she was feeling so down. He could always cheer her up when she was miserable.

She asked for a line, dialled the number, asked for Mr Yorke, and was put through at once. 'Hullo, Giles. Nicola. Are you tied up?'

'Just going off duty. All the time in the world.'

'I've just written off and accepted the post. I thought I'd tell you.'

'Terrific.' His voice deafened her, and she held the receiver away from her ear. 'That's really great. You've done absolutely the right thing.'

Well, it was nice someone thought so.

'And am I glad to hear it,' he finished. He had, in fact, begun to doubt that she would leave the Central and Andrew, and his first thought, when she came on the line, had been that she was going to tell him she had finally turned down the post. The relief that flooded him was tremendous, and he could have turned cartwheels in the accident unit office. 'I say, Nicky, how about a celebration, eh? You doing anything this evening?' Of course she is, you fool, he told himself. You ought to have learnt by now. She'll say sorry, no good, and it'll be Andrew, as usual.

'No, actually I'm not doing anything,' she said slowly. 'But how can we possibly celebrate, Giles? By the time we met we'd have to turn round and come back.' But it would be extraordinarily pleasant to be out with Giles, instead of thinking about Andrew and Gillian at Giovanni's. It might be almost worth meeting Giles halfway to the coast, even if only for a quick drink and a snack.

Giles was roaring away delightedly. 'Told you, you only just caught me. I'm off until eight o'clock tomorrow. So what I'll do is, I'll get the next train up, and then we'll have us a splendid night out. We'll go to the Country Garden, eat everything in sight, no expense spared. Have a bottle of wine, live it up for once. Taxis everywhere—no worries about drinking and driving, or parking. Let's have us a ball.'

'It would be lovely,' Nicola assured him wanly. 'We'll have a super evening. Nice of you to think of it.'

'I'll pick you up. Wear something to wow them. Six o'clock be too early for you?'

'Better make it six-thirty, perhaps.'

'See you then.'

CHAPTER FOUR

The American Team

THE COUNTRY Garden without Andrew was like a slap in the face, and Nicola felt worse than ever.

In a spirit of defiance, she was wearing her blue muslin. She felt totally wrong in it. It was Andrew's dress. Worse still, she saw Giles' eyes zoom in on the cleavage, and realised that the dress was every sort of mistake.

She must pull herself together. After all, Giles had travelled up from Halchester for the sole purpose of celebrating her new job. She was grateful to him—far more grateful than he'd ever know—and she had to snap out of her depression and enjoy the evening for his sake.

Pushing thoughts of Andrew entertaining Gillian at Giovanni's firmly to the very back of her mind—where, unfortunately, they continued to smoulder away threateningly—she watched Giles open the menu, and tried to work up an appetite.

'We're going to push the boat out,' he asserted. 'You're a senior registrar at last—remember?'

She was more cautious. 'In a month's time I shall be.'

'Oh, come on. It's only once in your lifetime you'll be able to drink to your first post as senior registrar, so you might as well make the most of it. Now, let's do justice to the food here, and the drink too. We'll have at least three courses, shall we? Maybe four.'

Giles' appetite had always been phenomenal, Nicola remembered. She must try to enjoy her meal as much as he did—here at the Country Garden that should hardly be difficult.

'To start with, you can have smoked salmon with egg mayonnaise,' he was saying. 'Or spinach and egg cocotte, game paté, or something called seafood gateau.'

She had to smile. 'I'm sure they don't mean fishcake,' she said. 'Not here. They must mean some sort of gooey concoction—shall we try it?'

'Right. Seafood gateau and then how about ginger pigeon with apricots and walnuts?'

'Fabulous.'

'Or you could have pheasant stuffed with oranges.'

'Either sounds fantastic.' Why was this so boring? Surely she didn't have to spend every evening with Andrew, or else go completely to pieces? What he was up to at this very minute with horrible Gillian was no concern of hers. 'Let's have pigeon, shall we?'

'Right. And a nice Hock?'

'Super.'

The seafood gateau turned out to be a creamy salmon mousse in a delicious sauce, dotted with shrimps and twists of cucumber. Even in her present mood Nicola forked it up with relish, and sipped the Hock with enjoyment—though it didn't actually quite come up to the wine Andrew usually ordered, she realised. Horrified, she did her best to deny what seemed a disgustingly mercenary reaction, and made another attempt to concentrate on what Giles was telling her about a restaurant near Halchester, Long Barn. Once she was down there, he'd take her straight along to sample its cuisine.

She smiled gently at him. 'That would be great,' she said, and tried to forget the way her stomach had turned over when he'd said 'once you're down there'. Ridiculous to feel that life would end when she left London. Her whole attitude was silly and juvenile, and she was going to put Andrew—and Gillian—behind her, have a brilliant career all over the world—and, what was more, enjoy this evening with Giles.

He was still telling her about Long Barn. 'It was converted by Justin Armitage himself, and there's an oak staircase in the hall open right up to the roof beams, with great windows overlooking the downs. Magnificent place. You'll go for it for sure, I know you will.' He couldn't wait to have Nicola with him down at Halchester. He'd take her everywhere, and they'd have the time of their lives. In the old days they'd never had any money—in the old days, he hadn't felt like this about her, either. But when she came down to St Mark's in a month's time, they'd really go places and do things. She'd soon forget about Andrew. 'You'll like Halchester, too,' he assured her, his enthusiasm rising. 'Lovely old cathedral city on a hill.'

'I'm sure I shall.'

'Quiet cathedral close, Georgian terraces and Tudor cottages all jammed in. And the sea as well. Wouldn't mind ending my days there, I can tell you.'

'Truly?' This had surprised her. Giles had always been restless, on the move, looking for the next opportunity.

'Quality of life,' he told her. 'That's what you learn about, down there. Work and sailing.'

She nodded.

Once he'd got on to the subject of sailing, he was unstoppable, as usual. He told her, in enormous detail, about his racing catamaran, its prospects for the year ahead. 'If you want real thrills, try sailing a cat.'

'I don't actually know that I do want real thrills,' she said apologetically.

'No, daresay it wouldn't be your choice. But you can find out—I'll take you out one day when there's not too much wind, and you can see how you get on.'

'Thanks. That'd be nice.'

'Not that I'll be able to take you often,' he said hastily. 'I'm trying to get the championship this year, and that means hard single-handed sailing most of the time.'

This was the Giles she knew.

'Still, I'll manage to give you a bit of a blow now and again. Do you good.' He scrutinised her. 'You're too pale. An indoor girl.'

'Thanks,' she said, sarcastically this time. At least Andrew had never told her she was an indoor girl.

He'd boobed. Blast. 'I don't mean it doesn't suit you.' She must be used to bloody Andrew paying her compliments, that was it. 'You look good. That frock—pow!'

In spite of herself she frowned. She couldn't bear it if he was going to start talking about her blue muslin. The first time she'd worn it was the first time she'd been sure that she could make Andrew notice her. But already those heady hopeful days had slipped into the past.

'The blue of the sea,' Giles said with an unusual touch of poetry. Spoiling it, he added 'You're too thin, though.'

She grinned. This was her old mate Giles, all right. At least he never changed. 'People really like it better if you tell them they're slim,' she pointed out. 'It means much the same, and it's better for their morale.'

'Sorry. But you are too thin.' All Andrew's doing, he was thinking. Andrew was tearing her apart. There she sat, eating delicious food, drinking the wine he'd bought, dressed to perfection—and miserable as sin. Pale, exhausted, tense. And there was nothing he could do about it. Not yet. Still, he'd found her this post a hundred miles away, and, praise God, she'd at least had enough sense to take it. What he had to do now was exercise that uncongenial quality, patience. It never came naturally to him, but he had to practise it now. He must stand back, somehow wait for her to pull herself together, and then help her to remake her life. Without Andrew.

The evening plodded miserably on, not helped by the fact that the waitress recognised Nicola, smiled cheerfully at her, and chatted in the friendly way she had done when Nicola had been with Andrew. It brought him too close again. Worse still, the girl was obviously intrigued to see Nicola with someone else, and eyed her speculatively from the serving table at the side of the room.

She was wondering, it was plain to see, what was going on. And that made two of them, Nicola reflected sourly.

Solidly, Giles talked on about Halchester, determined that Nicola should live in the future. Since she was equally determined not to brood over what Andrew might be doing with Gillian at that precise moment, she displayed enormous, and almost totally phoney, interest in Giles' accounts of the sailing club, the estuary and its complicated tidal system, and the astounding performance of his catamaran. Luckily for them both, the evening had to end early, so that Giles could catch the train to Halchester, and they took separate taxis away from the Country Garden. Nicola was thankful, when she reached her own flat and rang across to let them know she was back on call, to be needed in intensive care. Anything to stop her wondering about Andrew and Gillian.

The subject, though, couldn't be avoided. Andrew's meeting with Gillian—in the Central's main entrance, watched apparently by a thousand enthralled eyes—and their evening together at Giovanni's, scrutinised by half a hundred other diners, was the main topic of conversation in both general surgery and radiology. The hospital grapevine buzzed busily. Gillian and Andrew were joining up again. The divorce had been a mistake. She was coming to the end of her second Saudi Arabian contract, and she was planning to return to London and the Central.

Gillian was undoubtedly flourishing, she looked wonderful, the diners in Giovanni's reported. She was also wearing a luscious mink. A beautiful, fashionable and poised lady, not to mention an outstanding radiologist, she, like Andrew, was going to the top. She'd land another job in London whenever she wanted it, and be able to run a lucrative private practice, too.

Kind friends of Nicola's found themselves obliged to warn her of this, for her, doom-laden scenario. Never had she been more thankful than to be able to point out, with cool detachment and absolute truth, that she had already found and accepted the post at St Mark's. Her time at the Central was over in any case, she assured her relieved friends. She was already launched into the next stage of her career. Being with Andrew had been great, but they had both been well aware it was strictly a temporary arrangement, and now she had to leave him, she was relieved to know Gillian would be back in London again. Thank you. Next item?

Giles had been right from the beginning. Luckily she had listened to him, and St Mark's was waiting for her. Otherwise, where would she have been? Stuck at the Central, exactly as he'd warned her, still in a junior post, the cast-off girl friend. No job, no future. No Andrew, either. And the entire hospital watching her every move with avid, gossipy attention. No thank you very much. More than time to go. She had to think about St Mark's and her new job.

Easier said than done. St Mark's loomed ahead more like school at the end of the holidays than the summit of her ambition. She had to keep reminding herself that even before Gillian's reappearance, she had in fact half wanted the new post. There was a side of her that needed the promotion, the step upward.

Only not just yet. Not at the end of the month.

She and Andrew were together again, for the weeks that remained. She'd not been able—she hadn't even tried—to suggest there should be any break in their relationship. Only a few weeks now. Andrew had said nothing about Gillian, and Nicola would have died sooner than enquire. Their last days together were going to be as perfect as her love could make them. She dumped Gillian in a hidden corner of her mind, and gave herself to Andrew, pouring out all the love she had. It would so soon be over and done with.

'When is it you start at St Mark's?' he asked, one

evening as they were walking back to Harley Street.

'Two weeks exactly. Imagine. Me, a senior registrar at last.'

'Only your due.' He was short. 'I'm so glad for you, though.'

He was glad for her. Great. Probably, if the truth were known, he was glad for himself, too. Thankful to be rid of her with no awkwardness. Now she came to think of it, it had very likely been Andrew who had passed the word to Giles to look out for a post. The male trade union, as ever. It would account, too, for Giles' certainty. He knew she'd find herself redundant if she remained at the Central. That was it. Andrew had told him. 'It'll be nice to be working with Giles again,' she said in a brittle voice.

Undoubtedly Giles had fixed this post for Nicola, Andrew had recognised this from the beginning. But how much part had Nicola herself played? She'd known Giles, Andrew reminded himself, long before himself. Was it possible that underneath everything, it had always been Giles for her?

Giles Yorke, Nicola's true love.

Ridiculous. But one thing was very clear indeed. Whether or not Giles had been her only love, obviously he was going to be her next partner. So much for Andrew Ritchie. Now for Giles Yorke.

Nicola's final week at the Central vanished with the speed of Concorde, every day packed to its limits. It was typical, in fact, of all she valued in her London life, offering her, in one hectic week, everything she was going to miss once she was down at Halchester, and showing her—if she needed showing—that it wasn't entirely because of Andrew that she hated going. As her departure drew nearer, she felt worse about leaving. Yet she couldn't regret her decision to go. It had been right.

In general surgery, diaries were full to start with, and then in addition they found themselves with six Americans to entertain, stopping off in London, ostensibly for a rest before returning to their parent hospital, the Ocean Hospital in California, and staying with their old friend from the Central, Leo Rosenstein. They'd been lecturing and demonstrating to enthralled audiences all over Europe, and now they were turning themselves into tourists and doing London. Leo was going to show them. A year or two back, he, the perennial bachelor, had astonished them yet again by marrying Robert Chasemore's daughter Judith, a quiet and lovely girl with a bad medical history. The marriage appeared—a thousand eyes observed it critically whenever they had the slightest opportunity—to be a huge success. They used Leo's old flat still, round the corner from the hospital, and had as well a house down by the river at Richmond, where, this week, they entertained the American contingent, giving them wonderful food, and starting by taking them to Hampton Court for the day.

In addition, though, to being dined and wined and shown the sights, the Americans were to give one surgical demonstration of their technique. Strictly speaking, this was not entirely necessary, as Leo himself had both observed and assisted Milton B. Stone, the American surgeon, at the Ocean Hospital on his US tour the previous year, and he had since carried out the technique himself in London. However, the opportunity of having Milton himself to demonstrate it was too good to miss, and the gallery overlooking the general theatre was packed for the occasion with undergraduate and postgraduate students. Dr Stone had elected to be assisted, not by his own chief assistant but by Leo. This was generally felt to be a minor triumph for the Central, and in the gallery the students made sure the visitors from outer darkness were fully aware of it.

Preparations for the Americans had thrown general surgery into mild hysteria for the last two days, and this morning there was undoubted tension in the operating theatre. Technicians were snappy, as they set up the battery of electronics required for Milton B. Stone's surgery, everyone was slightly jumpy, and more than one of them had prayed earnestly to a God in whom they denied belief to stay with them and make sure their own personal bit of apparatus didn't fuse or blow a valve and let the English team down. The Americans had to be shown that anything they could do, we could do as well, if not better.

The theatre was full of trailing flexes and lights flashing green and red and yellow, and crowded with technicians, nurses, house surgeons, registrars, and the consultant anaesthetist, supported by Nicola. The room also contained the patient, hidden under towels, and bathed in arc lights.

This constituted the chorus and supporting players— not for nothing was the operating room known as the theatre. The automatic doors slid open, there was a brief expectant hush, and there stood the principals, Milton B. Stone and Leo Rosenstein, gowned, masked, their hands held high after scrubbing. High priests of surgery, if this had been the commercial theatre instead of the operating theatre, they might have been expected to process grandly towards their station by the table under the glaring light. Since this was a workplace in the Central London Hospital, what they actually did was tiptoe through the flexes, squeeze past the cabinets of blinking lights and festooning tubes, dodge the technicians, and somehow, still without having broken their sterility by actually touching anyone or anything, emerge at the centre of the maze, the operating table and the patient.

The patient, to no one's surprise, was ready for them, the registrars and senior registrars had seen to that.

Up in the front of the gallery, Lord Mummery leant forward. Once he had been the Central's senior surgeon, and in those far-off days Leo had been his house surgeon. Today, up from the country to watch the Americans, he was escorting Leo's wife Judith, soignée in a tawny tweed that matched her hair, and Sophie Waring, who had been Leo's secretary for years. Lord Mummery was devoted to them both, and instructed them throughout the proceedings, in his dominating teaching round voice, on the finer points of the American technique, to the considerable benefit—not to mention amusement—of the rest of the gallery. Most of them knew who he was, of course—he still examined for the Fellowship at the Royal College of Surgeons. Hearing his exposition was an unexpected bonus, though they dug each other in the ribs when he referred to Leo as 'the boy'. 'The boy's doin' all right, m'dear.'

Everything, not unexpectedly, went well, until finally the patient was wheeled away to intensive care, accompanied by Robert Chasemore, who had been present throughout, and Nicola. Meanwhile the surgeons went off to chat in the rest room and drink coffee, specially prepared today, in honour of the Americans, in an automatic filter borrowed from the heart surgeons, who had always taken the preparation of coffee a good deal more seriously than the general surgeons.

That evening, to take the load off Leo and Judith, Andrew had invited the Americans, together with half the Central, to drinks and a buffet supper, after which they would return to spend their last night in London, divided between Leo's flat and Dr Chasemore's flat, both of them just round the corner from the hospital.

Before this, however, Nicola had been delegated by her chief to take Janice Baker Vance, the only girl in the American team, and a radiologist, on a shopping spree. She wanted presents for her small son, left behind with her mother, and clothes for herself, 'as well as some of your lovely British china. That I must have.'

They went to Hamley's, and then on to Liberty's. Here Janice went temporarily off her head, buying four dreamy silk dress lengths, two for her mother and two for herself. In the basement china department, she crooned over Wedgwood and Royal Doulton, Crown Derby and Royal Worcester, and showed every sign of purchasing two terracotta garden urns, drifted ecstatically into the Victorian bazaar near by and was ravished by piles of nineteenth century hand-made lace. 'This is unbearable,' she said. 'I just want everything in sight. The problem is my baggage allowance.'

The urns had to be left in Liberty's. Not so the lace, however. Janice bought several metres, saying her mother would know how to make it up, and some of the men could carry it in their baggage for her. 'Mostly they bought perfume in Paris, and that's all. Gee, they sure don't know what they're missing—and nor do their wives.' She chuckled. 'Wait till they see what I'm bringing home. Now, china. I promised myself I'd go back with one of your real British tea sets. The problem is, which?'

Nicola enquired about colour schemes.

She was brushed aside. Janice, who was nothing if not decisive, had already reached her conclusion. 'Something very English, that's what I want. To remind me of all you lovely people and your lovely homes. Say, how about this? Roses. English roses from Royal Worcester—look, it's even called Royal Garden. That's the one for me. Mom is going to be real envious.'

While the china was being packed, they dropped in on the Eastern treasures, where Janice succumbed to a glittering evening coat. Finally, exhausted—or at any rate Nicola was exhausted, though Janice was bouncing still, and gloating happily over her purchases—they fell into a taxi and were decanted with their parcels at what Nicola felt was hardly her own lovely English home, empty as it was of antique lace, Royal Worcester china or Eastern treasures. The inventory had been done, she was packed and ready to leave the next morning, her successor appointed. Apologetically, she explained some of this to Janice.

'You're leaving the Central? Oh no, I don't believe it. I thought—' She bit off whatever it was she had thought and substituted '*Not* your last day, honey? And you've had surgery all morning and me taking up the afternoon. You should have told me, and—'

'It's been the nicest possible last day. I'll remember it. And what else would I have done? Just gone on clearing up and saying goodbye to everyone. And now there's this party—my send-off as well as yours.' Her send-off. Her last night had arrived. 'We'll have a coffee, and then we'd better change.'

'Coffee would be life-saving,' Janice agreed, sinking back into the depths of her armchair. 'I must say, this little apartment looks great to me, and not at all as if you were moving out.'

'It's much tidier and cleaner than usual, in fact,' Nicola admitted. 'I had a big turn-out. It looks a bit bleak to me, without my books and oddments, though.' A bit bleak was the understatement of the year, she reflected. The flat looked as bereft and lost as she herself felt. 'The coffee'll have to be instant, I'm afraid,' she said briskly, and departed for her tiny kitchen.

When she returned with two mugs of coffee, Janice was battling with tissue paper. Triumphantly she extricated the evening coat and held it out. 'I know I'm crazy, but I'm going to wear this. It'll be perfect with my harem pants.'

Harem pants were making a come-back that autumn, and Janice's were in flame-coloured chiffon, which, as she had predicted, set off her gold-embroidered ankle-length coat to perfection. Nicola, climbing ruefully into the only garment she had not yet packed, a severe and formal blue silk suit, to be worn tonight with the beaded and sequinned chemise she kept for grand occasions, felt a dowdy back number. No harem pants. No evening coat. Small wonder that, bored with her, Andrew was returning to Gillian in her mink. No doubt Gillian possessed dozens of evening coats, too, and drawers full of harem pants. Scowling, Nicola picked up the fluffy blue mohair stole that did duty as her evening wrap, and returned to the living room.

Ten minutes walk to Harley Street only, but Janice would hardly want to plod along pavements in her harem pants and her embroidered coat. Nicola reached for the telephone and summoned a taxi.

In the setting sun, Andrew's roof garden welcomed them. Two days ago, he had ordered from Moyses Stevens in Berkeley Square, at vast expense, extra plants for the tubs and bowls and huge flower arrangements to give a boost to his living room.

'No good imagining either of us is going to have a chance to arrange any flowers,' he retorted, when Nicola had protested at the extravagance. And now, she had to admit to herself, the plants looked as if they had grown there for ever, while the garden was giving its usual successful impersonation of a cottage plot in deepest Suffolk. The Americans were enchanted, and the party went with a swing. It was, of course, very much a surgical affair, and while it took place in Andrew's home, it was hosted jointly—by Andrew, Leo and Judith. She was a redhead, gorgeous in creamy brocade this evening, with emerald drops at her ears that matched the great emerald she wore next to her wedding band.

The party took off and was a roaring success, only ending because Leo firmly informed the Americans that they had to be up and away by seven-thirty in the morning in order to catch their plane at Heathrow. He scooped up, in the space of about sixty seconds, it seemed to Nicola, not only Judith and Dr Chasemore, but all six Americans. At one moment they were standing around in Andrew's big booklined attic room, glasses in their hands, apparently anchored for ever, talking, laughing, swapping tales of surgical mayhem, and the next they were pouring in a mob out on to the pavement, making for Leo's orange Mercedes or Dr Chasemore's grey Volvo, calling goodbyes and thanks to the night air.

Although she'd been looking forward to a few minutes alone with Andrew at the end of the party, Nicola found herself swept along with the US contingent, Janice's arm on one side, the burly American anaesthetist on the other. 'Come on, honey, you stay with us,' Janice said. 'Rob'll surely drop you off at your flat.'

'But—'

'No argument.' The anaesthetist was well away, Nicola had noticed it earlier, and now he draped himself over her shoulders. 'One thing I don' allow is argument from pretty ladies.' He nuzzled her ear.

Nicola would have liked to sock him one. However, in the cause of Anglo-American friendship she refrained. She bit back, too, the sharp retort one of the Central men would have received if he'd treated her like that. She must never be the cause of the visit ending on a strident note, with a fracas in Harley Street. A drunken brawl. While she fought down her increasing pugnacity, Dr Chasemore spotted her problem and rescued her at once. 'Come along, Nicola,' he said, disentangling her smoothly from the American. 'Of course I'll drop you. You two get in the back—Nicola, you come in the front with me, and direct me.'

He was so kind. He also happened to be her chief. Her provider of references from her teaching hospital for the rest of her career. She could hardly, now, say she didn't want a lift, thank you, she was going back upstairs to Andrew. It was not the sort of thing they'd ever done, and it would make her a laughing stock. Andrew would be furious with her—and in any case, who was to say he wanted to see her upstairs? He'd made no sign.

Dr Chasemore held the door for her, Nicola stepped

in. She caught a quick glimpse of Andrew shutting the remainder of the American party into Leo's Mercedes. Dr Chasemore shut the door of the Volvo, she was inside and Andrew was outside. Everyone was waving and shouting, her own tiny voice made no difference whatever, Andrew couldn't possibly distinguish it. Dr Chasemore let in the clutch, they slipped quietly along Harley Street and back towards the Central. That was the end. All over. Tomorrow she'd be on her way to St Mark's and a new life. Very likely she'd seen the roof garden and Andrew's living room for the last time.

'This the turning?'

'Yes, this is it,' Nicola agreed sadly. 'Thank you so very much.'

The Volvo drew in to the kerb. 'Best wishes for the future, my dear,' he said. 'Keep in touch, won't you?'

'I will indeed. Thank you for everything.'

Janice invited her, for about the hundredth time that evening, to California the moment she could fix a month off, wished her luck for the new job, thanked her for the afternoon's shopping—and then Nicola was across the pavement, letting herself into her own block, and the Volvo drew away. She didn't expect to sleep, but she was tired out, and dropped off at once. Early the following morning, though, she was awake. For the last time she lay in her narrow bed in the little flat round the corner from the Central, wishing that everything was different, that she didn't have to leave.

Why on earth had she listened to Giles? Why hadn't she followed her own instinct, taken the post in the orthopaedic department, and stayed in the same hospital as Andrew?

And stood by, watching him reunited with Gillian, living with her in the Harley Street house?

This morning she could even have borne that. Anything was better than leaving him. Perhaps if she'd remained at the Central she would have grown used to knowing he was Gillian's husband, that he might be her own friend, but nothing more. He could never be her husband. Not even her lover any longer. Simply her dear friend. Could she have lived like that?

She had no idea.

In any case, nothing of the sort was going to happen. By her own decision and no one else's, she had arranged to go to St Mark's. What she had to do this morning was to get herself there. Pack up and drive off into a new life. Try to be adventurous and forward-looking.

An hour later, she was driving out of London. On a senior registrar's salary, she reminded herself, she'd be able at last to afford a new car, instead of the almost vintage Volkswagon Beetle she'd bought dirt-cheap from Giles. Unless, that was, she wanted to spend her salary on evening coats and harem pants.

Who for? Who at St Mark's was going to care what she wore?

Oh Andrew, my darling love, why am I steadily driving away from you, when all I want is to be with you for ever?

Meanwhile, unsuspected by her, the telephone rang on, unanswered, in her empty flat. Because he couldn't bear to think she had finally gone, left the Central, without a word to him, Andrew listened to it ringing for far longer than was reasonable. Eventually, though, he put the telephone down, and squared angry shoulders. Like Gillian, Nicola knew exactly where she was going. She'd made it plain from the start that she was her own person, leading her own life, with a career to make. He thought back to the previous evening. There were the Americans, and there was Nicola, making sure they wouldn't forget her, making sure she was showered with invitations to visit them in California. Out shopping, for instance, all yesterday afternoon with Janice. Typical.

That Dr Chasemore, in whose flat Janice was staying, had detailed Nicola for this chore, mainly in order to give his daughter Judith a rest, didn't cross Andrew's mind. Nor did it occur to him that Nicola would have given anything to be able to detach herself from the Americans and the lift home in the Volvo. On the contrary, he assumed that she had planned it, as Gillian would have done. After two years at St Mark's, as far as Nicola was concerned, it would be next stop California, he told himself furiously. She was another Gillian, her eyes fixed on her future and her bank account. Presumably, he told himself cynically, he himself had originally held some sort of spurious glamour. A consultant, one of her teachers at the medical school and in the wards, sophisticated—compared with Giles, anyway—and, of course, with a far larger income. He had it made.

But here he had to break off. When he thought of Nicola, remembered how close they'd been, how loving, how much they'd shared, he was quite unable to believe his own nightmare picture. So why allow it into his mind? It certainly did nothing for his morale.

The fact remained, she'd gone. Of her own free will, and without a word of parting. Gillian had gone, and now Nicola had gone too, and he was alone again. Alone and desolate. No use pretending he didn't care. He did.

But he'd accepted from the outset that a day would inevitably arrive when Nicola would have to move on. Gillian had taught him that, and he wasn't going to forget it in a hurry.

There was going to be no repetition of the misery and shock he'd gone through after Gillian left, the months of hoping, of pretending to himself that their separation was no more than brief and temporary, that she'd be back, with him in London, the instant she'd completed her fellowship. There'd be nothing like that ever again. After Gillian he'd told himself that any girl he went around with he'd hold lightly, easily, wave goodbye with a quick gesture whenever the moment came.

So goodbye, Nicola. It's been great, and I'm sorry it had to end. Needs must, however. See you around.

CHAPTER FIVE

Harbourside Cottage

IN HALCHESTER, Nicola found Giles waiting for her at St Mark's. Sturdy, tanned from sun and sea air, outgoing and spontaneous, he was reassurance itself, and she began to feel slightly better.

Giles had booked her in for her first week at a pleasant little private hotel. After that she could find a flat, he told her, or a small house by the sea. 'The summer visitors have gone, and the agents are thankful to find tenants for the winter. There's a harbourside cottage you might like—several of us from the hospital have houses in the same terrace. I've got one myself, and I think it's super, but I must warn you, none of the cottages are anything to write home about. Plain and a bit knocked about, furnished for tough summer lets to families with rowdy kids. So don't feel in any way committed. Plenty of alternatives if you don't take to it.'

Typical of Giles, she thought gratefully. He'd already found her somewhere to live. She was incredibly lucky to have him here at St Mark's. If she had had to leave Andrew and the Central to be with total strangers, it would have been much harder to bear.

She went to see the cottage by the harbour, fell instantly in love with it, and took it for six months. The terrace, built in the previous century for fishermen and their families, ran down towards the quay, a chandlery, the harbourmaster's office, and a pub called the Dolphin. There were boats everywhere, their halyards rattling in the wind in the dinghy park, or swinging on moorings in the wide estuary.

'Fantastic, Giles. I never imagined anything like this. After London, it's terrific.'

89

'I hope you're going to be happy here,' he said. The words were trite enough, but his eyes examined her with clinical expertise, and he looked, she was irritated to see, both worried and concerned.

'I'm sure I shall be,' she asserted in a brittle angry little voice that carried no conviction. What she wanted to do was shout 'how *dare* you worry about me? I'm all right, do you understand, perfectly all right, and if I'm not it's none of your business anyway.' Not the sort of way to speak to Giles when he'd just found her this dear little cottage by the harbour. Why, in any case, should she suddenly want to attack Giles, of all people?

From somewhere within her depths the answer came back. Because he wasn't Andrew. Because he was there, finding her somewhere to live, working with her in the hospital, having coffee with her daily, meeting her in the lifts or along the corridors, when she wanted Andrew.

She had to get used to doing without Andrew. She had to get on top of her new job, learn to know her new colleagues, their strengths and weaknesses, and especially her new chief, Dr Ogilvie. And as if that wasn't enough, she had to move herself and her belongings to the cottage, settle herself in and make the place her own. So she would undoubtedly be far too busy to miss Andrew in the slightest.

She continued to find his absence unbearable. She'd known separation from him was going to be hard, but it was much worse than she'd expected. A constant dull ache under her ribs throughout her waking hours reminded her that Andrew had gone, and told her that she had no idea how to manage without him.

She wasn't alone, she reminded herself. She had Giles, her oldest and most supportive friend. But the ache within her was not interested in Giles, only in Andrew.

As she sat, tired and grimy, on the window sill looking across to the other side of the estuary, she longed for

Andrew to see her cottage. She wanted to show him round and tell him what she'd done. She'd spent the weekend moving in and arranging her belongings. Now she was in, and delighted with her new home. The cottage undoubtedly had potential, and she would make it truly her own. Her own tiny home overlooking the estuary. A private retreat, where she would be free to be herself, think her own thoughts, and forget about men and their unpredictable attitudes. All men. And that included not only Andrew Ritchie, but Giles Yorke, her new chief, Dr Ogilvie, Uncle Tom Cobleigh and all.

It turned out to be much more difficult than she had expected to ignore the men at St Mark's. They crowded round her, brimming with suggestions and invitations. She was a newcomer, and they found her fascinating. Obviously she had brains, she was able to handle her job with unflustered competence, and as a bonus, she had looks and sex appeal, instead of the hard brilliance of some clever women doctors. She turned them on, and their eyes pursued her, suggestive, inviting. Come to bed eyes, there could be no mistaking it. Eyes that undressed her with a look.

Nicola was furious. The incredible, outrageous nerve of the male animal. Their unutterable, boring cheek. She was their colleague, with, exactly as they had, a job to do, yet they had the unutterable conceit to suppose that if they chose to intimate that they were even mildly interested in her as a sex object, she would be flattered and eager.

Head high, she stalked the corridors, icily ignoring these leering apes who apparently supposed she had nothing better to do with her life than to set up in business as the hospital whore, that she'd be gratified to be offered the chance. She'd show them. They'd see.

They saw. 'Talk about *noli me tangere*,' they grumbled.

'You're right. Untouchable is the word.'

None of this stopped them trying. If anything, it served to whet their appetites.

Oddly enough, this unwelcome sexual attention had an effect Nicola had not allowed for. She turned thankfully to Giles, who could be relied on to treat her as a normal human being.

At once, this had the desired effect. They paired her off with him, and most of what it would have been ludicrously exaggerated to have described as sexual harassment ceased as if a tap had been turned off. She was, she presumed angrily, accepted now as Giles' property.

She had to remind herself constantly that she was resenting her colleagues for no reason at all. That they had greeted her arrival by trying to make the grade with her sexually, and had promptly desisted when they saw her pair off with Giles was mildly hilarious, but nothing else. So why was she so angry?

She knew the answer. Anger diverted her attention, helped her to overlook the unhappiness that dogged her days and nights in Halchester. Most of all her nights. By day she was occupied—and angry. At night she was alone and desolate, with no flaming rage to restore her. Separation from Andrew ate into her soul, and, just as Giles had warned her, she could find no way of coping with it.

Andrew hadn't even troubled to ring her, either, to see if she was going on all right. Out of sight, out of mind. Very likely he had far more important things to think about, such as Gillian. Remarriage. Probably he and Gillian were already living together in the Harley Street house, sitting in the long chairs in the garden where she'd been so happy, and making love there.

In December? She laughed sardonically. Time marches on. She was in Halchester, and what went on in London was nothing to do with her. She had done right to leave, and begin a new life. She set her lips into a thin line, and her blue eyes flashed with a diamond-hard brilliance that terrified her house physician and the nurses in intensive care.

Andrew could do as he liked. It was all one to her. What was definite was that she wasn't going to ring him to find out. She had never pursued him, and she wasn't about to start.

This blatant untruth pulled her up. Of course she had pursued him. What was more, she'd caught him. But once was enough. She'd done it, it had been enormously worthwhile, however unbearable now. But it was over. Finished.

Now was the testing time. If he didn't bother to ring her to see how she was, then that was it. There was no longer anything at all between them. Not even friendship.

Giles needn't think he had all the answers, either. He was absolutely wrong that she'd crumple, be unable to handle her loss. She'd grit her teeth and live through it. He'd see. They'd both see, Andrew and Giles. She'd come through, until one day she'd no longer care. One day she'd be free. One day. But when? When she was about sixty and approaching retirement, probably. Like her new chief, Dr Ogilvie.

She switched her mind rigorously into work and its quite different problems. Her new job was as interesting as she'd hoped, and she liked her chief. Dr Ogilvie, whatever Giles might say about him, was a pleasant and kindly man. Sound, too. Careful, and extraordinarily gentle and considerate with patients.

According to Giles, though, Dr Ogilvie was more or less senile, and should have been pensioned off years back. He was quite wrong, she found as soon as she began working with her new chief. True, Dr Ogilvie was occasionally a bit out of date, and if he erred it was on the side of caution. Giles, indeed, could have done with a bit of that himself. He was a good and thorough surgeon, but apt to be over-enthusiastic, too sure that surgical intervention was going to rejuvenate every patient. This was why he and Dr Ogilvie got across one another. Only to be expected, now she came to think about it, that Giles should claim that the older man was fussy, obstructive and cautious to the point of inertia.

In actual fact Dr Ogilvie was a good clinician, well ahead of Giles in that field, and a brilliant diagnostician. Unlike Giles, he refused to leap to conclusions based on intuition alone. There was a tremendous amount she could learn from him, and the fact that he was in some ways very oldfashioned was neither here nor there. He was precise, of course, a stickler for exactitude – and punctuality. And this was another reason why he and Giles didn't get on. Giles had never had much sense of time. If he was called out in the night, he'd cheerfully work through until dawn, but when he did finally go off duty, he'd sleep for hours—right through his alarm, often—oblivious of overdue appointments and out-patient clinics, ward rounds or committees.

Dr Ogilvie liked every day organised, everyone in the proper place at the proper time. Dosages, too, had to be checked and rechecked, both in metric and imperial measure. This particularly infuriated Giles, but Nicola quickly adapted to the habit. Giles, when he heard her checking like this with a new houseman, scoffed irritably. 'You're getting nearly as bad as old Fubbydiddles himself,' he jeered.

Nicola didn't care for his nickname for her chief, and was in any case annoyed with him for using it in front of the house physician. In her eyes, Dr Ogilvie was rather a lamb. Small, grey-haired, with twinkling brown eyes and a plain, round face with a ruddy complexion from years of exposure to the wind off the sea, he had a cosy presence that reassured patients. In her new bleak world, Dr Ogilvie was a comfort, and she wasn't going to encourage Giles to go round making jokes about him in front of the juniors. She liked working with him.

She was astonished, though, and put out, to find how much exhilaration and promise had vanished from her hospital routine, simply because there was no Andrew to be encountered round the next corner, in the canteen, or waiting for the lift. She did her best to ignore this, and settled into her job and her little cottage, telling herself how lucky she was, in both her hospital and her home. In the cold days of winter, she looked out from her windows across the estuary over mysterious grey seas fading into a grey distance, with only an outline here and there from the masts of a ship on a mooring. When she had arrived, the estuary had been filled with them, the air outside the cottage filled with the twang of rigging and halyards frapping against masts.

Christmas came and went, the accident and emergency department working flat out right through the holiday, so that she was able to tell herself she had hardly missed Andrew and the Central. She'd had a card from him—probably sent by his secretary from his list, she thought sarcastically—and had sent him one in return, a view of St Mark's sold in aid of the Friends of the Hospital, to show how routine a gesture it was.

Clumps of snowdrops made their intrepid appearance at her front door and down her garden by the sea wall, and she gloried in them. Her own flowers, in her own garden, and to hell with roof gardens in Harley Street.

The cottage was freezing—almost as cold, it often seemed, inside as out of doors—and especially hard to take after the heat of intensive care and the operating theatre. When she had time to light it and enjoy it, she could have an open fire in the big downstairs room, but apart from this she had only expensive and inadequate electric fires warming only a narrow space in their immediate vicinity. But she wore thick sweaters, padded trousers and lined boots about the house, and stared out of her windows at the wide grey seas, at the waves crashing and the salt spray flying at high water, or across the empty, deserted marshes at low water. Nothing, however freezing the weather, would have made her abandon her harbour-side home.

She was alone one evening in the cottage at the end of March, exhausted after a hard day, drinking coffee and eating a belated sandwich instead of lunch, tea and supper, when the telephone rang. She swallowed hastily, cursed inwardly, and reached for it. If she had to return to intensive care now, or go to the operating theatre again for yet another tricky emergency anaesthetic, she'd scream, she told herself. In fact, as she knew only too well, she'd do nothing of the sort, merely present her cool, calm, public face to the world. Competent Dr Lancaster, unruffled, calm, ready for action.

Andrew was on the line. Just when she'd finally given up expecting him to ring.

'Hi.' He sounded abominably cheerful, filled with amiable good humour. 'How are you getting on down there? Thoroughly settled in by now, I daresay.'

After over four months, he might well suppose something of the sort. She gritted her teeth. 'Yes, thank you,' she said politely. Stay with me, cool, calm public face. Don't abandon me now. I need you. 'I—um—I have this really charming little cottage by the harbour, you know. Giles found it for me, as a matter of fact. I feel I must have been here for ever.'

She did, did she? One in the eye for him, that was. Don't imagine I'm missing London, or you, or the Central, in any way, was what she meant. Right. He could take a hint as well as any man. 'I won't keep you. What I rang to say is'—he was efficiency personified, might as well have been discussing tomorrow's list with his houseman, she thought—'I happened to run into Michael Adversane at an editorial board the other day— you've come across him at St Mark's, I expect?'

'Er—yes, I have. Sure.' Nicola collected what remained of her wits. Michael Adversane, a surgeon in the children's department, with a slight limp. It was this limp, rather than his exceptional good looks, which had stayed in her mind, and she had asked a colleague about it, to be told that as a young registrar Michael Adversane had had to have a leg amputated. Something to do with a mountaineering accident in Nepal, her informant believed.

So Andrew knew Michael Adversane.

'Well, I had a drink with him, and he was telling me he'd acquired a sloop, a five-tonner, the fortunate bloke. He was asking me if I'd care for a sail one weekend.'

Andrew would be coming down to Halchester to sail with Michael Adversane. Excitement flooded Nicola.

'Naturally I said I'd like to, but there's not a hope I can get away in the near future.'

He wasn't coming.

'But then, of course, I thought of you. I told him you were down at St Mark's, and you'd done a good deal of crewing for me over the years, and suggested he might like to take you out. Obviously you'd be much more useful than me, as you're on hand, and you'd be able to fit in the odd evening or morning sail when the tide was right. Anyway, he said he'd be in touch with you, so I thought I'd better put you in the picture. It might not be a bad idea to remind him—I daresay there are plenty of sailing types around St Mark's more than ready to crew for him.'

'Oh yes, I'll look out for him, and remind him. Marvellous opportunity. Thank you very much for speaking to him.'

'Right. I'll leave you to make contact with him, then. Good sailing.'

The line clicked, and his voice in her ear was replaced by the dialling tone.

He'd gone. But at least he'd rung her, even if only in a routine way to arrange some sailing. Suddenly a mad elation took possession of her, as her spirits rocketed.

Giles would be furious with her for reacting like this to one perfectly ordinary telephone call.

Giles could get lost. Very likely, he was one hundred per cent right. She had to get over Andrew. But she wasn't over him yet. Hearing his voice had done things for her. She felt entirely different from the zombie who'd plodded through her days at St Mark's for nearly five months.

She picked up her half-eaten sandwich. It tasted wonderful. She took a sip of tepid coffee. Never had there been such coffee. She stretched luxuriously. Had she been tired, earlier? Gone. She was poised for action, ready to go, energy zooming from every pore. She wanted to sing and dance and run round the harbour.

She pulled on her anorak and left the cottage by the garden door. Out on to the path by the sea wall. Dusk was coming, and a mist from the sea. The wind off the water was fresh and damply salty.

The tide was coming in, filling up the marshes, little encroaching wavelets hissing and foaming quietly, pressing through the reeds and reaching out for the head of the creek and the far shore. High water in an hour or two, and her garden, instead of running down to the marshes, would be on the edge of the sea. Nicola strode out along the path, her feet touching the ground as though they were fitted with coiled springs, on which she could only bounce along. At any minute she might bounce off the top of the world.

She was alone with her intense joy, only the sea and the evening sky to share her happiness. Her heart sang, and the past receded, the present vanished without trace. She had no commitments, no anxieties. There was only tonight and the darkness and her love for Andrew. And his voice in her ears.

CHAPTER SIX

A Telephone Call

THE NEXT DAY, of course, brought with it its own problems. But nothing mattered. Nicola knew she could cope with whatever came along. The heavens could fall, or the rest of the department go raving mad. Whatever it might be, she'd manage effortlessly.

Or so she imagined. But she was unprepared for Giles. Capped and gowned, his gloved hands held in front of his chest to maintain sterility, he strode into the accident theatre to deal with an open fracture of the leg on a young motor cyclist who'd crashed that morning on his way to work.

Giles glanced round, checking. Entirely normal behaviour. Nicola, on her stool at the patient's head, was ready to receive his routine enquiry. 'Patient ready, Nicky?'

It failed to come. He was staring at her as though he'd never seen her before. 'What's happened to you? You won the pools or something?'

Could she possibly be looking so different? Gowned and behind a mask? In any case, she certainly wasn't going to mention Andrew to him in the accident theatre, with every ear flapping, and have him tick her off in front of them all. She lowered her eyes, watching the patient, adjusted the valves and rechecked the readings as obsessionally as Dr Ogilvie might have done, finally replying, in the coolest and most dismissive voice she could summon, 'Nothing at all has *happened*, as you put it. The patient is quite ready for you.'

'Thank you.' He'd have to leave it for now. 'Ready, sister? Right.'

Not a doubt of it, though, Nicola had to admit to

herself, she did feel marvellous. Perhaps it showed. Perhaps it was bursting out all over her. It was, however, nothing to do with anyone else, and she had no intention of discussing it over the operating table.

Giles was talking to the house surgeon now, and Nicola breathed an inward sigh of relief. With any luck he'd lose himself in the surgery, and forget whatever it was about her that had so astonished him.

'What we have to do this morning,' he was saying, 'is no more than a good wound toilet. Later on we shall have to embark on some rather fancy metal work, to fix these two portions of this broken shin bone together. Now, though, we're only really preparing for that day. We want to ensure there'll be some good healthy tissue on his leg. We have to examine the fracture site thoroughly and carefully, with the field free from bleeding for a while. Irrigation tube and sucker, sister, please. Right. We must fiddle about and make sure we get away all this dead tissue and the dirt that's got into the wound. Quite a long slow job, and not to be hurried. His future depends on a slow and steady cleaning up job at this stage.' His hands worked on, meticulously, while he thought about Nicola. He could read her like a book. She sat on that stool as if she was about to take off. Alert, blue eyes brilliant with elation, oozing joy from every pore.

Andrew had been in touch with her. Would she never learn?

A setback, too. Just when he'd been beginning to think she'd said goodbye at last to her old London life, had settled in at St Mark's and was allowing Andrew to slip into the past. Giles had even started to hope that she might be nearly ready to make a new life down on the coast with him. A life that would lead somewhere. To marriage, for instance, a shared home, eventually a family.

In the old days he'd never thought of Nicky like this.

Seeing her with Andrew had put the idea into his head, had forced him to realise that little Nicky Lancaster, whom he'd taken for granted for so long, who'd been around, pleasant, useful, good company when he felt like it, had matured into a very beautiful and sexy lady. Men's eyes followed her. She'd even succeeded in collecting, however briefly, Andrew Ritchie himself.

'Now I think this wound can be said to be surgically clean. Let's see the flow of blood resume. Good. Good. Excellent. That demonstrates clearly that the remaining tissue is healthy, and should heal well. So we come to wound closure. What do you suggest?'

The question was normal. But the angry eyes above the mask that suddenly stabbed into the house surgeon's skull were not. Unnerved, the houseman dithered. 'Er—um—simple skin suture, perhaps?'

He'd got it wrong. 'That would be a mistake,' Giles snapped back. 'He's lost too much skin for the edges of the wound to be brought together with a good blood supply. What we must do here is pack the wound, so that it can heal from the depths by granulation tissue. That should go well in a fit young bloke like this—that is his present state, isn't it, Nicky, I hope?'

'Yes, he's fine.' Everything was fine, in fact. The patient, herself, and even Giles, obviously lost in the details of surgical management. How mistaken she was in this belief Nicola was unaware.

Certainly Giles gave no sign of the uproar in his head. He was talking to the house surgeon again. 'If you'll start packing the wound,' he was saying, 'I'll rig up the traction. We have to bear in mind that we must be able to inspect the wound frequently to make sure it goes on free from infection.'

At last, with the leg in traction, the patient was ready to leave for the recovery room with Nicola, and by mid-afternoon, he was safely in the accident ward. Nicola called in to see him, and found him alert, pestering the nurses for the telephone trolley to ring up his girl friend, so that she could check on the condition of his bike for him. In short, he was doing well.

As she left the ward, she met Giles on his way in.

'Ah, Nicky. Just the person I wanted to see. Doing anything tonight?'

Damn. He probably wanted to spend the evening interrogating her, and then reading her the usual riot act over Andrew. Oh well, if he must, he must. Nothing to be gained by putting it off—he'd pin her down at some point, she couldn't keep dodging. 'Not actually,' she admitted.

'Good. I'll stand you a meal at Long Barn. Something I want to talk about.'

What on earth could it be? A ticking off about Andrew would hardly rate a Long Barn meal. So what was it?

Sister, at Giles' shoulder, was asking herself the same question. Long Barn, indeed. A meal there cost a bomb. Was he serious about Dr Lancaster, then, as people had been saying? Was he perhaps even taking her out to propose? She spread news of the invitation widely. Speculation grew.

In fact, Giles was busily warning himself against doing just this. Much as it went against the grain—impulsive, he liked to swing into action the moment a possibility crossed his mind—he told himself he must bide his time. Take it slowly. For the rest of the day he went on reminding himself. Don't rush your fences, Yorke. Be as slow and painstaking and cautious as old Fubbydiddles himself.

Still restive, however, he collected Nicola and drove to Long Barn. He'd had his own dreams about what might happen between himself and Nicola as spring moved into summer, and summer into autumn. The first stage of his plan was upon them, and he couldn't decide whether to put it into execution or not. Ever since Nicola moved into the harbourside cottage, he'd foreseen this moment arriving. When summer comes, he'd promised himself, and the rents go up, Nicky and I can move in together, share one rent between us. And then with any luck by the end of the summer the arrangement would have become permanent. She'd take it for granted. He watched her, wondering, uncertain. Would it be a huge error to suggest at this stage that they might share? He could easily, he thought reluctantly, lose all the ground he'd gained, be worse off than when she first arrived at St Mark's. If she rumbled him, his safe position as her old friend and support would be lost. Thrown away by his own impatience. Better play safe. Something would have to be done about summer lodgings, though. He reworded what he'd planned to say. 'What I wanted to talk about, Nicky, is that the moment is fast approaching when the harbour cottages go up for summer letting. You need to think about where you're going to live.'

Startled blue eyes met his. 'Already?'

His heart turned over. He longed to say 'don't worry, my love. I'll see to it. I'll take care of you for ever.' He swallowed the words, and said only 'Fairly soon, I'm afraid. From Whitsun, anyway.'

'That's a bit of a blow.' Nicola had known that some-time she'd have to think about moving out, but she'd imagined that she had until late May or early June to make her plans.

'Last year,' Giles was explaining, with a slightly wary expression that she was at a loss to understand, 'we all of us moved into one of the end cottages, and shared that, paying one summer rent between us.'

Nicola groaned. 'You're not seriously proposing that four of us should squash into one of those tiny cottages for the whole summer? Surely there's something else we can do?'

He longed to risk telling her exactly what, but

clamped his lips against the urge. It wouldn't do. Don't risk it, he told himself fiercely.

'How long do we have before we have to decide?' Nicola was asking.

Giles pulled himself together and told her.

'So you mean, if necessary, I could pay extra rent for May and September—more than I'm paying now, but not the full summer rate—and then only have to share, or find somewhere else, for three months, June, July and August.'

'That's right.'

'I'll think about it. Thanks for warning me. I'm afraid I hadn't realised it was so imminent.'

As soon as she was alone, Nicola began doing sums. The idea of moving in with the others failed to appeal to her. It wasn't that she didn't get on with them, simply that to move in together struck her as a return to the hugger-mugger living of her student days. It was not for this, after all, that she had left London. Halchester and St Mark's had been a sacrifice, made solely in order to bring her one step nearer a consultant post. It should at least be marked by a small step upwards in living standards, and the harbour cottage had seemed to be this. Spartan it might be, but it was her own little home with a view of the estuary and a garden running down to the sea wall. A place that she could occasionally kid herself had made leaving London worthwhile.

Nothing had made leaving Andrew worthwhile.

Could she perhaps keep her own cottage, and share it with one of the others? The physiotherapist in No. 3, for instance, was easy to get on with—they might be able to keep house together for three or four months. It might work. She could offer the physio the big front bedroom—Nicola always slept in the small back room with the windowseat and the view of the estuary and the boats on their moorings.

However, she wasn't going to give in and share with

anyone until she'd made a few enquiries. If she couldn't afford the cottage for the summer, she might be able to find somewhere else that wouldn't force her into sharing.

Unfortunately, she discovered, as soon as she started looking, that anywhere at all possible demanded the same high summer rent. The only alternative was to take out a mortgage on a leasehold flat. But she expected only to be at St Mark's for the two years of her contract, of which six months had already passed. No, she'd have to rent somewhere.

Slowly but surely she came to a decision to stay put. She did more sums, and then went to see the agent, on her day off, to enquire about the summer rent of her own cottage.

The sum horrified her. If she met it she'd have to say goodbye to the holiday on the Adriatic that she had been planning.

Summer on the coast would be quite something, she reminded herself, and she'd also have an opportunity to spend a couple of weeks with her mother and stepfather, and even fit in a week with her father and his wife.

More sums. By cancelling the Adriatric holiday and keeping her old heap of a car, which she'd intended to change for an up-to-date model, she could just manage. So that was settled. She'd stay in her harbour cottage and enjoy it. It would be worth it, even if every month's salary cheque did disappear into the cottage. There'd be sailing, too. Most of them stuck in London at the Central, she knew, would envy her summer by the sea.

What was more, if she crewed for Michael Adversane, there was always the possibility that one day Andrew would be there too, sailing with them. He was an old friend. If she hung on, one weekend when she was least expecting him—there he'd be. And that was something that wasn't going to happen if she went on holiday to the Adriatic.

If she'd only known, precisely the same hope was in Andrew's mind. He'd been struggling with himself. He still felt that Nicola had dropped him for the sake of her career. He spent long hours arguing with himself on this point. All right, he accepted that she hadn't found it easy to go. He had watched her, he'd known that, just as he had done himself, she had counted her remaining days in London with dread. When he asked her how long she had, she always knew to the very day. His own enquiries had been attempts to extract from her a hint of regret, some indication, however slight, that she might be hesitating. But she hadn't wavered. Not once. She'd clung to him in bed, sure enough. Five years earlier, Gillian had clung to him in the same way, before she'd gone off to the United States. She had hated going, so she assured him, but she'd never questioned the necessity. Her career, it turned out, came before everything. At the time, he'd respected her for her decision—but that had been when he'd imagined she felt the same way about medicine and a career as he did. The Fellowship, he'd agreed, was an opportunity too good to miss—secretly, though, he'd been shocked she hadn't refused it and stayed with him. But it was, of course, only for a year. A year was nothing.

A year had been the end. Gillian had gone, and never came back.

So that was how it was. And with Nicola it would be the same story. After all, sex, as Nicola herself had pointed out more than once, wasn't everything. Sex was great, sex was delightful, but there was no reason why it should last for years. Simply a lovely happening. A bonus, to be accepted as such, thankfully. Not a way of life. Not for a lifetime, either. Joy here and now, and then goodbye, and no hard feelings.

Goodbye, sure enough. And he was the one left with the hard feelings. Too bad. He'd keep them to himself. It wasn't the first time he'd had to do that—but it would be the last. No more lacerated emotions. No more loving self-centred girls. He was through.

And astonished by the strength of his own feelings. He'd known he was fond of Nicola, but this agony of loss was far more than he had been prepared for. He could do without anyone, when it came to it. Gillian, Nicola, any woman, however attractive, however loving, however much she became part of his existence—he could do without her, he promised himself. He prayed for the pain to recede soon, as it surely must, and in the meantime snapped everyone's head off, and lost weight.

He also fought a long-drawn-out battle with his hand, which led, apparently, a life of its own, and would in the evenings keep reaching out for the telephone to ring Nicola. No way. Going had been her own decision. He wasn't going to start running after her. That would be the final defeat. What a pathetic figure he'd cut, making an idiot of himself first over Gillian and then over Nicola, who had had the appalling taste and lack of discrimination to drop him for that oaf Giles Yorke. So she'd gone down to St Mark's. Let her stay there. Let her get on with it. Let her marry Giles, and take out a mortgage and start breeding, if that's what she wanted. It was all one to him. His own affair with her, extremely pleasant while it lasted, was over and done with. In the past.

If only the pain would slip into the past, too. If only he could forget the damned girl. If only he didn't ache for her unceasingly.

When Michael Adversane, after the meeting of the editorial board, had begun telling him about the boat he'd bought, it had seemed natural to tell him that Nicola was down at St Mark's and, he was sure, would be delighted to crew for him. He'd given her a good strong recommendation, as he knew he'd have to do before Mike would risk using her, surrounded as he no doubt was by sailing talent, and then he'd gone home, feeling better than he'd done for months. Talking to Mike about

Nicola seemed to have done wonders for his morale.

His subconscious, pleased, had promptly sent up a suggestion.

Cautiously, he considered it.

It would be only natural to tell her what he'd arranged for her. Under different circumstances he wouldn't hesitate. So why not? No one could read anything into a casual call about crewing for Michael Adversane in his sloop, could they? No one at all.

His hand reached out. He snatched it back. No need to rush blindly into anything. He ought first to work out what he was going to say.

He'd spent a most pleasurable ten minutes doing this, rejecting most of the phrases sent blithely up by his heart—singing a quiet little paean of praise to itself—and when he'd established a suitably non-committal formula, he at last allowed his fingers to begin dialling.

Well, so he'd reached her. But much good it did him, he thought morosely after they'd spoken. He'd been right all along. Just as he'd suspected, she was heavily involved with that clown Giles Yorke.

All the same, an unexpected thought surfaced, it had been nice hearing her voice.

Oh Nicola, I don't know how to do without you. I can't do without you.

'You'll bloody well have to,' he snapped aloud.

But the war went on, day and night, and he found he no longer knew what to do about her.

Perhaps, the idea at last began to insinuate itself, he ought never to have let her get away?

All right, he hadn't gone running after Gillian, but that didn't necessarily mean he shouldn't have pursued Nicola. His marriage had already been a disappointment when Gillian had left him, though he hadn't chosen to admit it. But nothing had been wrong between him and Nicola, except her departure. So why had he sat about at the Central feeling sorry for himself, instead of going after her? Why had he assumed that if she took a job somewhere else, and showed signs of thinking about Giles Yorke, he should spinelessly let events take their course?

Why on earth didn't he tear after her and change her mind back for her?

For the first time since she'd left, he grasped the fact that Nicola was not Gillian, though he'd been treating her as if she were. She'd never been in the least like Gillian, he informed himself, surprised. She was Nicola, his love.

And he'd let her walk out of his life without lifting a finger.

CHAPTER SEVEN

Another Telephone Call

MICHAEL ADVERSANE'S boat, *Lapwing*, twenty-six feet in length, was in his eyes easily the most beautiful creature afloat. He'd acquired her from a boatyard in the Solent at the end of the previous season, so this was the first year he had sailed her. She was traditionally built, of wood rather than fibreglass, had four berths and a tall mast reaching for the sky.

On the first occasion Nicola sailed with him his wife Jane accompanied them, leaving their small son with friends. Jane Adversane, almost as tall as her husband, was a sturdily built redhead who had only recently given up work at St Mark's to raise a family. 'I shan't be able to do much crewing for Mike this season,' she explained to Nicola, yelling over the roar of the outboard as they rocketed out to the moorings in the rubber dinghy. 'Young Freddie's proving a real tearaway. So just when Mike's bought this dream of a boat, wouldn't you know it, there I am, housebound.'

Gracefully, *Lapwing* stood out against the sky. Michael's eyes were alight with pride, and he took the dinghy along past the boat swinging on her mooring. 'Hasn't she the most lovely lines?' he asked, as he turned, cut the outboard, and came gently alongside.

They made the dinghy fast and climbed aboard. Half an hour later they were clear of the harbour, *Lapwing* seeming as if she were alive under their feet, cutting through the water as if she were as delighted as anyone to be out in the open sea. How Andrew would love sailing like this, Nicola thought. When would he come down? He should, not because she yearned to be with him, but because he'd enjoy it so much. The experience

110

was one he shouldn't pass up. She ought to tell him so. A resolve began to form.

The sail was an enormous success all round, but far too soon it was over, and they were ashore. Nicola thanked Michael enthusiastically.

'Enjoyed it myself,' he said. 'Glad you came.' Jane had gone ahead to collect the baby and see about lunch, while Nicola helped Michael to deflate the dinghy and stow it, with the outboard. 'We must do it again,' he added pleasantly, raised a hand in a quick farewell gesture, and turned off to the path up to the cliff top, where his home was.

Back in her own cottage, ravenous, Nicola cooked bacon and egg, drank quarts of coffee and ate a mound of toast. Then, tired but triumphant, she leaned out of her bedroom window, felt the wind on her face, and realised she'd actually enjoyed herself without Andrew. Of course, it would have been even better if he'd been there. She shook her head irritably. Her thoughts were back where they invariably ended, with Andrew. Hardly surprising Giles found her obsession with him ridiculous. She was behaving like an infatuated teenager. At least today, though, there was no pain. Only this longing to share her sailing with him.

She could ring him. Now. It would be no more than a return call. Very likely he was re-established with Gillian in the Harley Street house, but one call, one fearfully casual call about sailing, could hardly embarrass him, could it? She could thank him for introducing her to the Adversanes, tell him he must somehow make time to get down for a sail himself. No harm in that. She brought her head smartly in from the window and reached for the telephone.

He was there. He answered. And once again, simply the sound of his voice made her feel as if she were back on cloud nine for ever. 'Hullo, Andrew. It's me, Nicola.'

As if he didn't know. At the first syllable he'd recognised her voice, and his spirits had soared. Nicola was ringing him. She was here on the end of the line.

'Is it all right to talk? Or are you busy?'

All right to talk? It was all he wanted from life, to talk to her for ever. 'Of course,' he said, his voice clipped, his emotions successfully hidden. 'How are you?'

'Oh, I'm fine, thank you. How are you?'

'Fine.'

There was an infinitesimal pause, which they broke simultaneously.

'What I rang to—'

'Busy, of course. You know how—'

Both of them stopped abruptly.

'Sorry,' Nicola said. 'You were saying?'

'No, no. Carry on.'

Nicola began again. 'What I mainly rang for is to thank you for arranging for me to sail with Michael Adversane. I've been out today, and it's been super.'

'I'm so glad.' She'd rung to thank him, out of politeness. Not because she wanted to be in touch, or because she was missing him, or for any of the mad reasons he'd somehow managed to believe in the few seconds between first hearing her voice and answering her.

Nicola was being very careful. She must go cautiously, not overstep the mark. Not risk over-enthusiasm. She must tell him the truth, that she knew he'd enjoy a sail in *Lapwing* as much as she had done herself, but she must on no account seem to be putting pressure on him to come down to Halchester and see her personally. The object of ringing him, she'd told herself before she'd begun to dial, was to have a brief chat, and finish. Her aim was simple. To reopen communications—without being caught at it. She wanted to be able to ring him, to hear his voice, without any especial significance being attached to it. Never mind Gillian. She had no more importance. This had been her astonishing discovery. Half a loaf was infinitely better than no bread.

Friendship with Andrew was second best, but it would have to do. It was far better than nothing.

All this in mind, she finished thanking him, urged him to sample *Lapwing's* delights for himself one weekend, made a brief remark about St Mark's and Dr Ogilvie, and said a quick goodbye. Andrew wasn't to know that when she put the telephone down she sat there, her heart brimming with love, sending him silently all the messages she hadn't allowed her lips to frame. Messages like *'Oh Andrew, it's wonderful to hear your voice. I do love you so.'* Or *'Darling Andrew, ring me back, please ring me back and tell me you still love me. Me, and no one else.'*

Huh. She should be so lucky.

Anyway, she decided as she drank coffee and pretended to study an article in the *Lancet*, it had been great hearing his voice, and perhaps he would ring her back. Not today or tomorrow. In a week or two. Or a month or two. And if he didn't, she'd ring him. But she'd have to let six weeks or so go by before she did anything like that.

Even so, the prospect sent her into St Mark's the next day with electricity sparking off her dark hair and a lift in her step.

Giles took one look at her and knew—except that he assumed it was Andrew who had rung her. He'd dated her. And the stupid girl had agreed to meet him somewhere. Nothing else could have lighted up those blue eyes so that they shone like twin beacons.

In the Central, Andrew was not so easy to read, though the general theatre was certain something had happened. He was in a very odd mood all week, they agreed. Edgy, snappy, yet with a concealed air of triumph.

Some girl, they decided. At last he'd got round to replacing Nicola Lancaster. He'd been like a monk since her departure. Now he'd begun a new affair, that must be it. That would account for the triumph—and the snappiness, too. He didn't want to be in the theatre, operating. He wanted to be chasing this new girl.

They were right on that point. He wanted to take off for Halchester. He was in turmoil, and irritated with himself because of it. One telephone call from Nicola, and his emotions were in chaos. The power she had over him terrified him.

It wasn't simply that he wanted her back, either. What was shaking him to his foundations was the sudden certainty that seized him as he replaced the telephone when she rang off. He was going to go down to Halchester and get her back.

No matter what it cost. No matter how involved she was with Giles Yorke. She was his girl, and he was going to get her back. He must have been out of his mind ever to let her go. He must be mad now, he reminded himself caustically. After all, much as he missed her, he wasn't proposing to throw all his hard-won experience down the drain and embark on a second marriage, was he?

If he went down to Halchester after her, that was what he'd have to mean. He couldn't claim her back from Giles, that pillar of respectability, labelled so unmistakably 'husband-material for Nicola', and then not marry her himself.

Marry Nicola? Why not?

Furiously he tried to remind himself of the failure marriage had turned out to be with Gillian. He was never going to risk another fiasco like that. Never. What he was beginning to understand, though, was that he himself might have been another sort of idiot to try to assess his relationship with Nicola by anything that had happened to him and Gillian.

Back to square one, then. He would go down to Halchester the minute he could fix a couple of days off. What's more, he wouldn't stop at that. He'd begin courting her. Seriously. And if she could be persuaded to marry him, then they'd be married.

He'd been ridiculous to have made such a scene in his head about Nicola's move to St Mark's. Of course she had to follow her career wherever it led, as he would have done at her age. But what was two years at St Mark's compared with a lifetime together?

If only he wasn't so busy. If only he could get away tomorrow—or even at the weekend. Not a hope, though.

Leo would have to be away just now. He was lecturing in the USA and, unusually, he'd taken the senior registrar from general surgery with him as demonstrator. So they were short of their senior registrar as well as Leo himself, and, to cap it all, this would have to be the year when Andrew had his own staff problems. His house surgeon, on paper, should have been a gift from the gods. Brilliant, a high flyer with a tremendous future ahead of him—provided, that was, he could be bothered to get there. He was bone lazy. He didn't have to try to succeed, he could do that by giving little more than half his attention or his time—or so he had found during his student days. As a house surgeon it was a little different, but he hadn't cottoned on to that. In Andrew's opinion, he wasn't safe unsupervised. He was too fast, too certain, too uncaring. Too inexperienced, and with it, too apt to leap to clever lightning diagnoses that were occasionally dangerously wrong. As a surgeon he was verging on the spectacular. Quick, deft, one move ahead of his chief all along, a joy to work with. It was what might happen before the patient reached the table that gave Andrew sleepless nights. He was afraid to move from the hospital unless the overworked RSO—the senior resident, whose next post would be as a consultant—was free to take over more or less full time. With his own firm on take-in for the coming week, there could be no question of so much as one night away.

Frustrated, he turned over the pages of his diary. Hopeless. To be as tied as this, with his years of seniority, was ludicrous. Yet there it was. He couldn't leave with anything approaching an easy mind.

The following weekend?

Hell, he was down to speak at a conference in Westhampton, and do a teaching round on the Sunday morning, as well as joining the discussion panel arranged for Sunday afternoon. Another weekend lost. What's more, after getting the RSO to cover for him from Friday night until Sunday night, he couldn't expect to clear off again the next weekend. On the contrary. He'd have to offer to take some of the load. So that was that. Three weeks before he had any chance of getting down to Halchester.

Wait a minute. What about the Westhampton weekend? That shouldn't be too far from Halchester. Less than fifty miles. He consulted his road map. The trip was nothing. All side roads, which was a pity, but he ought to be able to do it, provided he didn't lose the way, in an hour and a half. Saturday night, and back at Westhampton for the ward round on Sunday morning. The chairman had offered to put him up, so he'd have to get out of that somehow.

Hey, no—much more to the point. What about inviting Nicola over to Westhampton? She'd enjoy the postgraduate weekend, and she could come with him on the round—just as she always used to, he thought with a pang—and between sessions they'd surely be able to snatch a little time alone.

As the plan grew on him, he started to feel much better. Optimism grew fast, and had he been able to reach Nicola at that moment, perhaps the weekend might have been the success he dreamed of. But he was called to the hospital, and when he eventually rang Nicola, two days later, he'd had time for second thoughts. What would have been an enthusiastic and unmistakable invitation reached Nicola as a somewhat starchy request to a former junior to attend a useful conference at which she would be bound to learn something, and where her former teacher would be a principal speaker.

Even so, Nicola was over the moon. A whole weekend at a conference with Andrew. His invitation must mean something. At the lowest, continuing friendship.

Of course, Gillian might be there with him. In her mink, no doubt. That would turn the weekend into one of the more hideous experiences of her life. Even this, though, could be treated as a step forward, and she must be prepared to face it as such. At the very worst, she'd know where she was, where she stood with Andrew. She'd have to grit her teeth and accept the fact that the most she could expect in future was an undemanding long-term friendship. She'd value even that.

She wrote off and booked herself into the conference. Papers came back, with the full programme—on which, she was delighted to see, Andrew seemed to feature as the star attraction.

Once more her blazing eyes and bouncy walk conveyed the exact truth to Giles. He cursed inwardly. Was the poor silly sucker never going to learn? Useless to say anything. Not his place to interfere, he told himself, and did precisely that at the first opportunity. 'Heard from Andrew, then, have you?' he asked, almost through clenched teeth.

Nicola turned surprised blue eyes on him. 'I have, as a matter of fact, though why you should—oh, did he get on to you as well about the conference?' An acute sense of disappointment engulfed her. He hadn't rung her only. He'd probably been on to anyone who'd ever been on his staff now residing within a hundred miles of Westhampton. Very likely the chairman had asked him to drum up support for the meeting.

'Conference?' It was Giles' turn to be puzzled. 'What conference?'

Nicola's morale surged back. Once again she was on top of the world. 'There's a weekend conference at Westhampton, starting on Saturday the 16th. Andrew's one of the main speakers. He suggested I should go to it, so I've booked myself in.'

Giles assimilated this, his fury renewing itself. As he'd thought, Andrew was making a fool of Nicola again. Taking advantage of the conference to have a bit on the side. The perfect weekend, no doubt. Main speaker at a postgraduate conference, with an adoring girl friend in tow. Disgraceful. Unkind and inconsiderate, too. Taking advantage of Nicola's vulnerability again. Somehow, Giles told himself, he was going to put a stop to it. Enough was enough. He wasn't going to stand by any longer, watching Nicola destroy herself like this. He'd never let on to her, but he'd heard in detail from his own friends at the Central about Gillian's reappearance in Andrew's life, and he'd congratulated himself then on the fact that he at least had seen what was coming, and had more or less made Nicola take the post at St Mark's. Just in time, that had been. Now he was going to step in and save her from herself again. He approached the problem as if it had been a new and difficult piece of surgery. Not a false move. Cool and quietly assessing every step, all reactions monitored before they occurred, almost. 'What,' he enquired carefully, 'is the conference on? Who else is speaking, apart from Andrew?'

Relieved to see he had recovered from his temper and was now taking a sensible interest, Nicola told him. '*Surgical Management—The Team Approach*, it's called.' She hunted in her desk, produced the programme they'd sent her, and handed it to him.

He read it through conscientiously. 'Interesting,' he commented finally.

'Yes, I thought so. Should be worthwhile.'

'I agree. If I can get cover for the weekend, I might go with you.'

Nicola was aghast. To have Giles around was not at all how she had seen the weekend. On the other hand, if he wanted to, he had a perfect right to attend. And maybe Andrew had meant her to spread the news of the conference round St Mark's. She had been silly earlier, imagining a postgraduate conference would be like two days on a desert island with Andrew. Of course Giles must attend if he wanted to. And in fact, her more anxious self surfaced and pointed out, if Andrew did happen to have Gillian with him, she herself would be thankful to have Giles around as cover. 'Yes,' she agreed. 'Why don't you come too? You'd better write off and book fairly quickly, in case they're getting full up. Want to take the address down while you're here?'

Giles took the address down.

Nicola didn't know what to think. One minute she'd be genuinely thankful Giles would be there, the next he was not only the last person she wanted in Westhampton, but the last person Andrew would want either. What had she done? What would Andrew think—in the wholly unlikely event, that was, that he retained any of his old feelings for her? If only she could stop Giles.

No way. That evening she took an angry walk round the harbour, blind to the setting sun in its copper and gold, blind to the ebbing tide and the dusk taking over the marshes. What could she do?

She must try to be dispassionate. Clear away the emotional clutter. She was going to a conference with Giles, but she didn't want to be stuck with him, or give the appearance of being partnered by him. That was the problem.

The answer stared her in the face, and she couldn't imagine why she hadn't thought of it earlier. Amazing what a brief spell of clear thinking could achieve.

She had to bring up reinforcements—make up a party from St Mark's. She'd left it a bit late, of course, but there was still time. She reached for the telephone.

CHAPTER EIGHT

A Surgical Conference

ON THE SATURDAY of the Westhampton conference, the party from St Mark's set off rather grandly in Dr Ogilvie's ancient Bentley, driven by its owner with Nicola beside him to map read. In the back, two housemen and an accident registrar muttered in subdued voices. After all Nicola's machinations, Giles hadn't in the end been able to get away, as until midnight he had to cover for the RSO, on a week's leave. So much for her manoeuvres. She might have left well alone—though Giles was still hoping to attend the ward round and the afternoon discussion on Sunday.

Dr Ogilvie, as soon as Nicola had told him her plans for the weekend, had also demanded to see the programme. He knew the anaesthetist who was to speak immediately after Andrew, he told her. He rather thought he might accompany her. 'Dominic can stand in on Saturday for both of us, and I'll cover Sunday.'

Startled, Nicola, with collapsing spirits, had felt obliged to offer to forgo the Sunday meeting herself and remain at St Mark's, so that both Dr Ogilvie and Dominic—her opposite number in the hospital—could go to the conference.

Luckily he'd brushed her offer aside. 'One day's quite enough for me.'

And now here they were, on their way. Nicola had dressed with enormous care, trying to look at one and the same moment like Dr Ogilvie's capable senior registrar and Andrew's sexy love. Early that spring she'd bought, extravagantly in Halchester's top boutique, a smokey grey suede suit with that season's blouson jacket. This she had donned, with a pin-tucked blouse of the same grey, and a black and white striped scarf for emphasis. There was the senior registrar, sure enough, but what had happened to the sexy girl friend?

She would have to do as she was. She tried, with no success whatever, to still her bubbling excitement. This morning she was going to see Andrew.

And by this evening, an unkind voice from her depths reminded her tartly, she'd be back in Halchester, very likely knowing the worst.

'Don't you think so, Nicola?' Dr Ogilvie repeated patiently.

'I'm so sorry. I was working out the route, and I'm afraid I missed what you were saying.' She must pull herself together. Concentrate.

'I was saying I thought the wind would drop once we're inland a bit.'

'Hope so. It must be nearly gale force. Not much sailing today, that's for sure.'

Her chief, who was not a sailing man, laughed unkindly.

'A bad forecast, too,' Nicola added.

'There you are, my dear.' He beamed at her. 'We made a wise choice, setting off inland, while in the sailing club those fanatics'll be standing about, fuming.'

At the Westhampton hospital, arrows directed them to the postgraduate centre, where there was to be sherry before the first paper. The party from St Mark's trooped in like schoolchildren behind Dr Ogilvie.

There, slightly to the left of the reception table, where staff were booking new arrivals in and pouring sherry, Nicola at once spotted Andrew, looking immensely senior in a smooth navy pin-stripe, a whiter than white shirt and a Central tie. He was holding a glass of sherry, which he detested, and talking to another expensively suited individual who had an air of harassed bonhomie, and whom she rightly guessed to be the chairman of the conference.

Dr Ogilvie, as a distinguished visitor, was pounced on immediately by the organising secretary and borne off to be introduced to the chairman. Since he was good at looking after his own staff, he beckoned Nicola over. The chairman began introductions.

'No need,' Andrew told him. 'Dr Lancaster and I are old friends.'

Old friends, indeed. That was one way of putting it. She didn't know whether to be pleased or indignant. Mainly, of course, she was in a haze of enchantment. To be standing there, next to Andrew at last—it wasn't all she asked of life, not by any means, but it seemed to be undiluted joy. Not that she had any intention of allowing anyone to guess how she was feeling.

She became very clipped and correct, introducing Andrew and Dr Ogilvie to one another in the most formal manner imaginable, and telling each of them about the other's most recent papers in the *Lancet*.

The two of them began talking about Andrew's coming speech, while Nicola sipped sherry cautiously and listened. They were soon joined by the anaesthetist from Westhampton, who would speak after Andrew. It turned out—she might have guessed it, Nicola thought—that he had once been Dr Ogilvie's registrar, and he made much of his former chief, insisting on fetching him another glass of sherry.

After that the meeting began, and Nicola found herself ensconced on an easy chair in the front row, alongside Dr Ogilvie.

Andrew's paper went down very well, as she had known it must. Even so, she felt like a proud but anxious mother whose child had managed to survive a hideous ordeal—though as far as could be seen Andrew himself remained unruffled throughout.

The anaesthetist followed him, then the medical specialist, and finally the consultant in physical medicine from the rehabilitation unit attached to the hospital.

There would now be a break for lunch, the chairman informed them, after which the speakers would re-assemble for the afternoon session as a panel to answer questions and hold a discussion. Lunch would be available in the refectory, on the other side of the car park, and there would be a cash bar.

There was a clatter of chairs as the bulk of the audience headed for it.

Dr Ogilvie rose more slowly to his feet. 'Well now, my dear,' he was saying comfortably, when the chairman and the anaesthetist appeared at his side.

'I hope you'll join the speakers at my table for lunch,' the chairman said.

'That's very kind. Are you sure I—'

'Shan't sit down without you,' the anaesthetist stated.

This was the signal for her to melt unobtrusively away, Nicola knew, and she backed discreetly.

Dr Ogilvie was having none of it. 'If you've room for Dr Lancaster too,' he said, 'We'd both be delighted to join you, wouldn't we, my dear?'

Hardly another consultant would have bothered to look after her like this, Nicola thought, touched— though here she perhaps underestimated the effect of piercing blue eyes, long legs and a figure even more ravishing than usual in the smokey grey suede.

'I can easily—' she began.

The chairman, eyeing her a little as if she had been the Sunday joint, interrupted. 'Of course there's room for Dr Lancaster,' he bellowed, following this by a ribald and sexist comment that Nicola, in deference to Dr Ogilvie, allowed to pass.

Soon, led by the organising secretary, Andrew and the physical medicine consultant, they were straggling across the car park, Nicola bringing up the rear—the chairman having been collared by the medical consultant, who was arguing earnestly with him over some point in the afternoon session. I am the only non-consultant in this group, she told herself, half ruefully, half complacently. Her main emotion, though, had nothing whatever to do with her lack of consultant status.

She was not only here, in the same hospital—or, strictly speaking, at this moment the same car park—as Andrew, but shortly, within ten minutes or so, or however long it took them to swallow the pre-lunch drinks the assiduous chairman had offered, she would be sitting down at the same table, eating the same meal.

Was there the slightest chance that he might sit next to her?

Not likely. He, the main speaker? And she, the interloper from below the salt—which, today, would presumably put her next to the organising secretary, and furthest away from the chairman and Andrew.

She had overlooked two points. The chairman was undoubtedly taken with her, and Andrew was a highly capable fixer. It was he, in fact, with an eye to the main chance, who'd suggested Dr Ogilvie's presence at the chairman's table, intending to see to it that Nicola came with him. He hadn't, as it happened, needed to intervene there, but he wasn't going to miss a trick now. To her intense disappointment, he kept well out of her orbit as they drank sherry, but materialised at her side as they moved towards the table.

'Come and sit next to me, Nicola. Dr Lancaster and I are both from the Central,' he informed the chairman. 'We've a lot to talk about.'

He could say that again, she thought, in a trance of delight, missing the extreme irritation displayed by the organising secretary. So much on cloud nine was she that even the chairman's reply left her untouched, though it would normally have raised all her hackles.

And then she was sitting next to Andrew, with the

physical medicine consultant on her other side, Dr Ogilvie and the anaesthetist opposite.

Lunch was nothing out of the ordinary. Cold meat and salad, followed by rhubarb pie accompanied by cream that on tasting she discovered to be evaporated milk. The usual hospital catering.

Her conversation with Andrew could not be described as anything but mundane, either. With the chairman next to him, and Dr Ogilvie opposite, chipping in to their remarks whenever they felt like it, there was no possibility of any personal contribution going unheard—nor, given that particular chairman, unrepeated. Brandished to the table at large.

In spite, though, of the extreme ordinariness of the meal and the conversation, Nicola had never known a more exciting lunch. As she sat, shoulder to shoulder with Andrew—the table was not large, and with two extra they were a little crowded, so that now and again grey suede brushed navy pin-stripe—she felt she might easily expire from sheer happiness. To be reunited with Andrew, even in this unpromising setting, gave back all the meaning to her life.

From time to time, their eyes met briefly—more than briefly, they were only too well aware, and the chairman would have been on to it, and come out, inevitably, with some lewd comment. Andrew was experiencing an overwhelming longing to throttle him. A good, capable surgeon, he'd always been tiresomely convivial, specialising in blue repartee, and today he'd overstepped all bounds, in Andrew's eyes. Mercifully, Nicola was being astonishingly patient with him. Here she was, sitting next to him at last, and suddenly he knew for sure what had been wrong with his life all these months. Simply her absence. Their eyes met, and slid hastily away. But they both read, each time, the same signal. Here we are, together again. Life is complete.

'Are you staying overnight?' Andrew asked. 'Coming

to tomorrow's sessions as well?' he added quickly, feeling the chairman's eye swivel.

'I'm coming tomorrow, but we're driving back to Halchester tonight,' Nicola said.

'One day is enough for me,' Dr Ogilvie explained across the table. He paused. 'Dear me, I might perhaps have phrased that better.'

'You might,' the chairman agreed. 'But we'll overlook it. We're a thick-skinned lot.'

Andrew gave Nicola a sharp kick.

Dr Ogilvie, who in fact had meant exactly what he had said, forbore to apologise further, adding only that it was their own fault for insisting on dragging him on to the platform for the afternoon's panel. 'I come to have a gentle snooze in my old age, rousing from time to time to hear one of you impart a few words of wisdom, and what do you do to me? Make me work my passage.'

'You're not getting out of it at this stage,' the chairman assured him.

'No, I was rather afraid not. Tomorrow, though, I shan't be here.' He smiled benignly. 'And you won't get me to pretend I'm sorry. But Nicola will be back, with our other senior anaesthetic registrar, I'm glad to say. I'm standing in for both of them, so let's hope it's a quiet Sunday for once.'

The talk turned to weekend casualty figures, while Andrew sipped his coffee and wondered whether he'd be able to detach Nicola from this other bloke tomorrow, and get her to himself after the conference ended. Should he offer to drive her back to Halchester? They could have a meal on the way.

'Giles will be coming too, tomorrow,' Nicola remarked. 'He had hoped to come today, but the RSO's away until this evening, and he had to cover for him.'

Andrew clamped his teeth over his offer.

Nicola was trying to make herself ask about Gillian. It was ridiculous to be sitting next to Andrew like this, and to be too scared to find out whether he and Gillian were living together or not. She needed to know, and who better to ask than Andrew himself? None of her friends at the Central would so much as breathe either his or Gillian's name, presumably because they were afraid of upsetting her, and she hadn't wanted to go behind Andrew's back to find out. She had her pride, and her loyalty too. But now here they both were, and she ought to ask him, put an end to uncertainty.

Somehow, though, she didn't. They were so close, so happy together, she couldn't bear to break into it by mentioning Gillian.

The afternoon meeting began, and Dr Ogilvie joined the panel on the platform. Nicola had a number of questions ready, she didn't intend to sit there in the front row tongue-tied and silent, but she needn't have bothered. Her chief was determined to show off the standard of his department's staffing, in the person of his senior registrar, and he kept feeding her with opportunities to shine. 'We had a case very like that,' he began. 'We were worried about the residual effects of the longer-acting anaesthetics. The patient—' he broke off. 'Dr Lancaster can tell you more about this than I can. Dr Lancaster, would you care to detail the measures we took on this occasion?'

Nicola was on her feet for nearly ten minutes.

Another question about anaesthesia, this time concerning patients with pre-existing chest disease requiring surgery, and again Dr Ogilvie drew Nicola into the discussion, and when she sat down after her admittedly high-powered exposition, he presented her with an unmistakable bouquet. 'Quite so. But I think I should add that Dr Lancaster has been over-modest in her account. Her personal experience and application of the Central's regime contributed greatly to our ultimately successful management of this case.'

Nicola went pink, Andrew looked as if he would like

to cheer, and the chairman was clearly flabbergasted. 'Thank you, Dr Lancaster,' he said blankly. 'Next question?' He looked round the audience as if he expected one of them to get up and bite him.

At the end of the meeting, though, when they were all drinking tea, he invited Dr Ogilvie and Nicola back to his home for a drink.

'Don't want to hang about.' Dr Ogilvie was emphatic. 'Many thanks all the same. Kind of you to suggest it, but we've a fair distance to cover, and none of it on a motorway. There's a gale blowing up on the coast, too, so I'd rather not be late back. Be off, shall we, my dear?' Collecting Nicola with a glance, he put his cup and saucer down on the table and turned on his heel.

'Thank you so much,' she said hastily to the chairman, who was looking crestfallen.

Andrew twitched an eyebrow in her direction. 'See you tomorrow, then?'

'Oh *yes*,' she agreed at once, in tones much more heartfelt than she knew, so that Andrew was cheered. Perhaps there was nothing in those notions of his about Giles, after all. Pity he hadn't fixed up something about tomorrow before she left. Never mind, he'd see her in the morning before the ward round, make a definite date.

CHAPTER NINE

An Emergency Call

IN HALCHESTER the night was noisy, with the gale force wind blowing hard, and Nicola expected the sound of the gusts buffeting her window to keep her awake. However, in spite of her excitement and her anticipation of another day at Westhampton, she was also exhausted, and drifted much sooner than she realised into a sound sleep, deaf to the increasing battering the harbourside cottage was taking from a wind whose force strengthened as the high spring tide surged into the estuary.

It was dark still when her telephone rang. Drowsily, she put on her bedside light and reached for the instrument. 'Dr Lancaster,' she announced sleepily.

It was not intensive care, but the accident unit. The RSO would be glad if she could come over. A trawler with a crew of three had sent out a Mayday call before abandoning ship. The rescue helicopter was out searching for them. One man had been badly injured before they took to the life raft.

'On my way, tell the RSO.'

The wind was hurling rain against her window with so much force it sounded like hailstones spattering the glass. She pulled on jeans and shirt, followed up by a thick jersey, her waterproof sailing trousers and jacket and her sou'wester, thrust her feet into sailing boots and a spare pair of shoes into her pocket, and let herself out into the uproar, praying that the ancient car would start. Since it was a reliable old heap, if slow and about as noisy as the storm itself when it got going, it started at once and chugged solidly through what seemed like walls of water and hurricane winds to St Mark's.

'Glad to see you,' the RSO said. A thoracic surgeon, tall and unflappable, he was a tower of strength around the hospital. 'The chopper's picked up the three casualties, and it's on its way. By all accounts the outlook's pretty grim. One has a chest injury plus plus, another's full of sea water and the other's probably gone already. They're doing mouth-to-mouth, but we're going to need full resuscitation stat. You and I had better go up into the chopper before off-loading, I think. So keep your gear on for the time being. No point in getting soaked to the skin before you start.' Normally addicted to well-pressed trousers and immaculate white shirts, he was wearing a pullover and baggy corduroys under an antique Burberry, with green Wellington boots, and looked more like a local farmer delivering a load than the Resident Surgical Officer of St Mark's Hospital.

Two porters in dripping yellow rain capes came through the automatic doors and began shaking themselves like wet dogs.

The RSO called across to them. 'Keep your oilies on, lads. You're going to need them.'

'Out to the helicopter pad, is it, then?' the younger asked at once, his eyes alight.

'That's right. And the patients are going to need very careful handling as we get them out—straight on to tilting trolleys. We'll have to—'

Two more porters arrived, and the RSO broke off, began again at the beginning. Nicola left him talking to them, and went along to the resuscitation room, where she found the house physician, Jamie Alston, with the registrar, Dermot Barry, and two staff nurses.

Dermot smiled at her. 'You been out with the life boat or something?'

'The RSO and I are going out to the helicopter pad with the porters and the trolleys,' she explained. 'So I'm not stripping off until we get back.' She pulled off her sou'wester and pushed her hair off her face. 'I'm steaming already, though. It's like a Turkish bath in here.'

'Want me to come out to the pad with you?' Jamie volunteered. Twenty-four, he looked more like seventeen still, and had an endearing puppy-like eagerness for any new experience.

'No, you stay here with Dermot and check the life support systems. We've two badly injured coming in, and one almost certainly DOA. One's a chest injury.'

'The RSO's asked the thoracic registrar to come in,' Dermot told her.

'Oh, has he? Good. In that case, we're going to be reasonably well-staffed for the chest case, aren't we? I reckon, then, unless when we see the cases we need to change our plans, you'd better go in with the RSO and stay with the chest injury, Dermot, and I'll stay with Jamie and the other one.'

'Right. Now, I've checked our equipment, and everything the RSO asked for—is there anything else you'd like me to be doing while you go out to the pad?'

'What about provision for warming? I know we may not want to, or even need to, but—'

'This is supposed to be British summer time. Flaming June, and all that. They ought not to be dangerously—' He broke off. 'You're right, though, of course. I'll make sure it's all present and correct, and ready for use.'

'Core temperature at once, obviously. Jamie, make sure the low reading thermometers are to hand.'

A noise as though the building was coming down on top of them filled their ears and drowned further speech. The chopper had arrived. Nicola pulled on her sou'wester again, tied it firmly under her chin. 'See you,' she mouthed, and went back to the reception hall.

Here the RSO, now wearing a villainous fishing hat above his Burberry, joined her, followed by the sister-in-charge.

The automatic doors opened for them, and they lowered their heads and belted out, rain blowing horizontally into their faces. They pushed through the downpour, against the hammering gusts of wind, and over to the helicopter, just settling on the pad. Brilliant lights cast long wavering shadows from the machine and from their own figures as they splashed through rivers of water.

The rotors stopped, a door opened, a figure appeared, and a helping hand was held out to Nicola as she climbed up into the cabin, the RSO on her heels.

An hour later, they were still fighting to save two lives. The third crew member, as they had feared, had died before reaching land. The skipper was half-drowned, and shocked. His heart was suspect. The mate was the man with the chest injuries, and they were extensive. When they'd first seen them both in the helicopter, it had looked to Nicola and the RSO as if any hope of saving either of them was verging on lunacy. But now, although they had a long way to go, it was beginning to seem possible that the mate might make it as far as the operating table.

About the skipper, Nicola was less hopeful. They'd somehow got him through the early stages of resuscitation, but the problem was that his heart was not taking the strain. They had had to defibrillate, and now he was on a pacemaker as well as a ventilator. In other words, he was on a total life support system. Without it he would have been dead. He had not regained consciousness, and Nicola was anxious to prevent brain damage—which could never be reversed—but she knew only too well that her own efforts might have begun too late, and his brain starved of oxygen before he'd been taken out of the water. His lungs must have been well and truly waterlogged, and the oxygen supply to his brain might have been inadequate for far too long. Just how inadequate it had been was what she didn't yet know.

The RSO, his white coat bloodstained, came into the cubicle. 'Nicola, could you spare a moment?'

'Sure. Get me back in here stat if you're bothered,
Jamie.' She followed the RSO out into the corridor.

'I'm taking my lad to the theatre—they're getting it
ready now. Thing is, I'd like you to come with me, if you
can. Dermot's OK, but it's going to be dicey. The patient
needs a good deal of work done even to patch him up for
the next week or two, and his lungs have taken a pasting
from sea water as well as the hoist—that's what started it
all. He was injured getting the trawl in, when the hoist
swung round in the gale and crushed him. It disabled the
vessel at the same time—that's when the skipper sent out
his Mayday call. My lad's in a pretty bad way generally—
no worse than yours, though, so if you think you can't
leave him, no hard feelings. But I'd like to have you in
the theatre with me.'

'I'll be there. If you can just spare me Dermot here for
five minutes, while I brief him. I'll send Jamie through to
you in the meantime—all right?'

'That's my girl. Thanks very much.'

In the theatre it was a long haul. But they didn't have a
death on the table, and the patient left for the recovery
room in better condition than Nicola had at one stage
believed possible. It was another hour, though, before
she could leave either him or the skipper—both of them
now in intensive care. By then, to her vague astonishment, the time seemed to be coming up for eight o'clock.
At eight fifteen, Dominic was to collect her. He was
driving them—herself and Giles—to Westhampton.

Hah bloody hah.

Her lovely day with Andrew. Gone with the wind.
Cancelled. Wouldn't you know it? Why had she ever
taken up medicine? And if she had to take it up, why on
earth had she chosen to work in an accident unit? She
could have wept.

Instead she dialled Dominic's number. 'I'm at St
Mark's still,' she told him. 'I won't be able to make it
today, after all. Don't come round to collect me, I'll

have to be here most of the morning, I reckon, even if nothing goes wrong. You get off.'

'Are you going to be able to manage, or would you like me to forget Westhampton and come in?'

'No, it'll be all right. Everything's under control, just a bit hairy. We're coping, though—and I haven't called the old man out yet, so we've still got him in reserve if anything else horrible blows up.'

'Blows is the word. What a damn shame you can't come, though.'

'Isn't it infuriating? At least I had yesterday. Enjoy yourself—and take care. Mind the gusts on the uplands and don't forget to dodge falling trees.'

'You bet. No way am I going to be admitted to add to your workload, I assure you. In fact, I think the wind's starting to moderate.'

'Tell Giles for me, will you? And if you have a chance you might apologise to the chairman of the meeting for me—and to Andrew Ritchie.'

Dominic was intrigued. 'You must have been moving in exalted circles yesterday, duckie, if you need to do anything like that.'

Nicola was apologetic. 'I was with Ogilvie, you see. I had lunch with him at the chairman's table, believe it or not.' She hardly believed it herself any longer. Already yesterday, with all its joy, seemed a long, long way away. 'They'll be expecting me again today—I said I would be coming. I had to sit in the front row next to the old man, in the morning, and then in the afternoon they hauled him up on to the platform to join the panel, and I was left alone in my glory in a front row easy chair, consultants for the use of. You'd better plonk yourself down in one, announcing you're Ogilvie and me, both. Try and cover yourself with distinction in the discussion.'

'I must say, Nicky, even if you had only the one day, you seem to have had yourself a ball. Hope I'm as lucky, but frankly I doubt it. See you this evening, anyway.' He rang off, and Nicola went back to intensive care.

When she returned to the cottage it was mid-afternoon. At St Mark's, she'd been too much involved with minute-by-minute care of the two dangerously ill patients to spare more than a brief pang for what she was missing. Now it hit her, and she didn't know what to do with herself when she remembered what today might have been like if only she'd been able to go to Westhampton. Being with Andrew yesterday had been like being reunited with her other half. And she'd happily assumed, then, that today would be a good deal more than a repeat performance. Today might easily have ended with herself and Andrew alone together, over a meal in a country pub. He might have driven her back to Halchester, in fact. Be with her at last in this little harbourside cottage.

What was more, she thought, and her heart gave an ugly lurch, she had not even found out where Andrew stood in relation to Gillian. She'd been with him yesterday, sitting next to him all through lunch, and she'd failed to find out. And now here she was, back on her own, as uncertain as ever whether Andrew was free, or remarried, or simply living with Gillian while they worked it out.

So there she was, in her old conflict, when yesterday she could so easily have discovered a few actual facts. She could have been dealing, now, this very minute, with a situation that was at least either one thing or the other. She would have known whether it had to be friendship only with Andrew, or whether there was a chance still of much more than that.

Of course there was much more than friendship. Sitting next to him yesterday had made that plainer than ever. She was sure there was more for him, too. His eyes hadn't met hers with nothing in them but easy friendship. His eyes had held as much meaning as her own.

So where did that get her? Was she prepared to have an affair with him on the side, whatever he and Gillian were doing?

Unfortunately she was. To do so went against her instincts and her commonsense, but she knew she was as much in love with him as she'd ever been, and she would have gone to him any day or night, Gillian or not.

And what that meant, she reminded herself furiously, was that she had been right to tear herself away from the Central and Andrew, to come down to St Mark's. What was more, she'd been right to stay away. To keep out of Andrew's orbit. To avoid him. For the simple purpose of self-preservation. Never mind the ethics of having—or trying to have—a relationship with him when he was living with Gillian, she knew she dared not do it. She wouldn't be able to stand the pace.

Just as Giles had always told her, she wasn't made for that sort of existence. She wouldn't be able to survive it.

Who said she wouldn't?

She wasn't as vulnerable as Giles always imagined. She wasn't some frail plant. She was tough as they come. She'd come through a stiff medical training, where, face it, everything was weighted against women. She'd achieved that. She'd achieved her present post. So who was to say she wouldn't be able to survive—what was more, enjoy—a lot of loving with Andrew, whether he happened to be married to someone else or not?

Come to that, why did she suppose that if it came to it, she would always lose out to Gillian?

Why shouldn't she change herself into one of those women who successfully entice husbands away from wives? Why assume that if Gillian wanted Andrew back, she had to have him?

These thoughts, although remarkably distasteful, were amazingly exciting, too, and Nicola began to gain a little confidence. Perhaps she had in the past paid too much attention to what Giles and a lot of them at the

Central had told her about Gillian's place in Andrew's life. All right, he'd loved her once, and he'd been broken up when she left him. But since those days he'd learnt to love her, Nicola Lancaster. He had loved her genuinely, Nicola knew that, whatever Giles might tell her. And yesterday he had seemed still to love her.

Perhaps he loved both her and Gillian. There was no particular reason why he shouldn't. His past love and his present love. Then he had a choice to make.

And if she had any sense at all, Nicola told herself furiously, she'd be in there fighting to see he made the right choice. There was no reason whatever why she should feel she had to stand back, resign her interest in him, simply because Gillian reappeared on the scene. She ought to have more confidence in herself. More confidence, too, in the power of their shared love, her own and Andrew's. Get up and fight, Nicola Lancaster. Go in and get your man back.

Energy and zest surged back, and Nicola, who among other things, had thought herself worn out, set to and made a fire in the living room and cooked herself a meal. In the flickering flames, the room was friendly and welcoming, and she ate her supper in front of the fire, and tried to plan a campaign to get Andrew back.

After supper, in the firelight, she grew drowsy, and slipped into pleasant dreams, half sleeping and half waking, in which she and Andrew seemed to be living happily for ever after, working at the Central together and living in the house in Harley Street. Her decision to fight to get him back had ended her conflicts, and she was at peace.

She began to think about an early night, and decided not to make the fire up, but to go to bed instead.

The door bell rang.

For a mad moment she thought it must be Andrew, come to see her at home because she hadn't been at the conference.

Disappointingly, her visitors proved to be merely Giles and Dominic, full of the day's events. She put another log on the fire, produced mugs of coffee, and they sat round talking about the cases they'd seen on the ward round, and the discussion at the afternoon panel.

'A shame you weren't able to get away, after all,' Giles said, though this was not in the least what he was thinking. He'd been relieved she'd had to miss the second day at Westhampton. Andrew had been too much in evidence, and Nicola's absence from the scene was a gift from the gods, though he had no intention of allowing her so much as a glimpse of this reaction of his.

'I made your apologies,' Dominic told her. 'You must have made an impression yesterday—they seemed to be quite shaken you weren't going to be with us. Particularly,' he added, eyeing her suspiciously, 'Andrew Ritchie.' Something on the go there, he suspected, though when he'd tried to pump Giles he'd got nowhere.

'I asked after Gillian,' Giles said.

Nicola gasped, but controlled herself at once, hoping that neither of her two inquisitive visitors had noticed. Here, naturally, she was out of luck. Both of them had recorded the sharp intake of breath, and the involuntary flinching. Recorded, and filed away for future consideration.

'Oh yes,' she said with a coolness that deceived no one. 'And how is she? Back from Saudi Arabia, I suppose. Has she found a post at the Central? Of course, she must have done, she'd be bound to.'

'Gone to California,' Giles told her, his eyes probing.

'California?' This was unexpected, and for a moment Nicola was out of her mind with delight and relief.

As Giles could see only too clearly. 'That's right.' He was going to scotch this nonsense once and for all. 'Got a post at the Ocean Hospital, and a lucrative private practice as well.'

'And some sort of dream house, swimming pool, the lot,' Dominic added. He'd been impressed.

'So if you ask me,' Giles went on deliberately, and only he knew he was lying in his teeth, 'it won't be long before Andrew joins her. She's working away to find him a suitable post, and once she lands it for him—California, here I come.' He gestured spaciously, watched Nicola, and was anguished. It was for her own good, he reminded himself. He couldn't allow her to go on tearing herself apart like this. He had to put a stop to it, and a quick, clean cut was much the kindest in the long run.

But this was the short run.

Nicola rose to her feet. 'I'm for an early night, if you two don't mind,' she said. 'I was up at four.'

Dominic apologised and made for the door, followed by an uneasy, half-triumphant Giles. His motives had been the best, he assured himself, back in his own cottage. What he'd said had obviously hit her hard, but that simply demonstrated how absolutely necessary it had been to say it. It was for Nicky's own good. She couldn't go on like this. It was up to him to put a stop to it, and he'd done so. In the end she'd thank him.

CHAPTER TEN

Giles

UNTIL he grasped that Nicola was not going to be at the conference after all, Andrew had been on a high to end all highs. He knew he'd not only done well as a speaker, but that it was mainly due to his own efforts that what could easily have been no more than a run of the mill postgraduate meeting had turned into a huge runaway success. All this was nothing, though, once he knew Nicola would not be there to savour his triumph. Refusing the chairman's repeated offers of hospitality, he drove grimly back to London. Flat, let down, lost—he had to face it—without Nicola.

He argued with himself all the way back to Harley Street. All right, so today had been a bitter disappointment, but he'd recovered from disappointment often enough before. Too bad Nicola hadn't made it, but the poor girl did work in an accident unit. That she should fail to get away was only to be expected.

But he hadn't expected it at all.

What he had to do was think about their next meeting. As soon as he could grab even half a day, he was going down to Halchester. He'd tell her he loved her for ever.

During the next week, he didn't have a free half day, and though he tried to ring Nicola more than once, he missed her each time. It was Saturday before his opportunity came at the usual monthly editorial board of the *Journal of Surgical Management*. Michael Adversane was there, and over the buffet lunch that preceded it, asked when Andrew was coming down for a sail.

'Only wish I could. I've thought about it often enough—trouble is, there never seems to be any time.'

'Why not drive down with me today, after we finish

141

here? Spend the night, and have a quick sail before breakfast? Tide'd be right, and you could be back in London by midday.'

'Tempting.' And that was the exact truth, though Mike would never know just how tempting his offer was.

'Let's give it a whirl.'

'I'd have to slip back to Harley Street for some gear, as well as ringing someone to cover for me.'

'If you show your nose in Harley Street, there'll be a sheaf of messages thrust at you, and we'll waste hours. Why don't we do a bunk from this place, and telephone from a call box on the way down, avoid getting held up by anyone? I'll lend you some gear.'

Like a couple of truanting schoolboys, they were driving down the motorway soon after five-thirty. They'd done their telephoning from the suburbs, though Andrew had not yet rung Nicola. He'd do that from the Adversane's, and with any luck they'd invite her round for dinner, and for the sail.

Luck, however, was not with him. He was sitting thinking comfortably about Nicola, when Michael breezily remarked that the two latest candidates from the Central to join them at St Mark's had been a resounding success.

'You mean Nicola?' Andrew was delighted.

'That's right. Charming girl. Capable, too. And Giles Yorke, of course. We've had him for almost two years now—he'd have been due to move on this autumn, but we're hoping to keep him permanently.'

This was less pleasing news. Andrew had imagined Giles would be leaving for another post in a few months' time. 'You're keeping him permanently?' he repeated.

'We've asked him to stay on for an extra year in his present post, with a view to stepping into Bagnold's shoes when he retires next year. Bagnold's the district's general surgeon. I don't think you'll have met him. An Anselm's man.'

'No, I don't think I've come across him. So you think Giles Yorke will get a consultant post next year, at St Mark's.' The information jarred him, and he was ashamed of himself. He ought to be pleased—Giles had been one of his students, after all.

'He and Nicola,' Michael remarked chattily, 'are a fairly settled pair. So hospital gossip says, anyway. We're rather hoping, as a matter of fact, that when Giles gets this post of Bagnold's, they'll be able to marry and settle down, and we'll end up by keeping both of them. Neat, eh?' Michael, his eyes on the road, missed Andrew's hastily controlled jerk forward in his seat and the grimness of his expression, and remained unaware of the blow he'd dealt him.

Andrew's dreams fell apart. For the second time round, he reminded himself bitterly, he'd been dropped by the girl he loved. There must be something about him that didn't hold girls. But why had he been such a fool as to expose himself to this heartbreak twice, when he'd so often vowed he never would again?

For heartbreak it was. Useless to deny it. He was angry as well, furious with Nicola, but he ached with the pain of losing her. He didn't see how he was ever going to get over it.

Goodbye, my darling Nicola. Goodbye for ever, damn you to hell. Oh, my darling love, how could you do this to me?

You can get lost, though. I'll show you. I'll learn to live without you and enjoy it, too. You wait and see.

Only a minute or two earlier he'd been planning to ring her as soon as he reached Halchester.

The whole purpose of coming down with Mike for this sail on *Lapwing* was to see Nicola, to sail with her. For them to be together.

All gone. Forever.

'Useful,' he heard himself remark shortly to Mike. 'Staffing never gets any less of a problem, does it?' He switched the conversation to new appointments at the Central and the manoeuvering that had accompanied some of them, and then to surgery. He talked rather brilliantly, in fact, for the remainder of the evening, and agreed with apparent zest when Michael suggested an early night in order to make an early start. No one could have suspected that instead of anticipating the morning's sail with eagerness, he was dreading yet another reminder of his lost dreams.

'A night cap?' Michael offered. 'Brandy? Whisky?'

Andrew chose whisky, and downed it faster than usual. Soon afterwards he went to bed. Not, he imagined, to sleep. But here he was wrong. This was, after all, the end of a heavy week, and he was exhausted as well as miserable. In the middle of telling Nicola what he thought of her, he dropped off.

If he'd only known it, she felt she'd just come through one of the worst weeks of her life. Following so quickly on the happy day she'd spent at Westhampton with him, the news that he was leaving the country had come as a shattering blow. Worse even than the week after Andrew had first spent the evening with Gillian and she herself had decided to leave the Central, worse than her first week at St Mark's, when she'd missed Andrew acutely almost every second of every hour, and her body had sent up an unending scream of anguish. Nine months ago, that had been. Nine months, or a lifetime. And now she discovered that Andrew was not only joining Gillian, but leaving London. Going to the USA. Probably she'd never see him again. Certainly she'd never have him at the end of a telephone line, even as a casual friend. She could hardly ring California pretending it meant nothing. She was losing him.

She ought to have faced it from the beginning.

Somehow, she didn't quite know how, she got through the week, looking tense, biting—most unusually for her—people's heads off left and right. Dr Ogilvie had been perturbed, and had asked more than once if she was well?

She was perfectly all right, thank you.

Was something bothering her?

Nothing at all.

Giles had been horrified. He'd never foreseen that his words would have quite this devastating effect. He wanted to weep for her, his poor darling Nicky.

Ought he at this stage to take back what he'd said? Tell her that as far as he knew, while Gillian undoubtedly was in California, Andrew had no intention of leaving the Central or of joining her anywhere? Nicky was suffering. He ought to tell her. As it was, he could hardly bear to catch sight of her round the hospital, pale and strained. Deeply unhappy. And because of what he'd said.

But if he took it back, she'd suffer more. The fact that she'd been so completely thrown by what he'd told her only went to show how dangerous this love of hers for Andrew was. Just as he'd always said, Giles reminded himself. Andrew was bad for her. She couldn't cope with him. Everyone knew he was never going to marry Nicky. To interfere at this stage, to tell her, so to speak, that Andrew in fact was still available and at the Central, would only be to postpone the inevitable. One day she'd have to suffer as she was suffering now.

No, he'd been right in the first instance. A short, sharp shock. Which could be followed by a steady convalescence.

Throughout the week Giles was gentle, supportive, loving. Vaguely, Nicola was grateful to him for his kindness and understanding. Dear Giles, always there when she needed him. She took him far too much for granted. She ought to value him more than she did. He was trying so hard to help her, and he didn't once say that he'd warned her from the beginning that this would happen, or something like it, and she wouldn't be able to handle it. But he had warned her, again and again, and he'd been right. She couldn't handle it.

He even went so far—though it went against the grain—to offer to take her for a sail in his catamaran. She knew this represented real sacrifice—he was intent on winning the championship, and he preferred to sail alone and perfect his handling of the boat. Twice this week, though, he offered to take her with him. Since he'd wanted, as usual, to sail before breakfast, she'd refused each time. In her present state of misery, the last thing she could face was the scramble to tidy herself up after sailing, followed by a rush on duty—probably late, too, as he never had any sense of time. But when he urged her yet again to sail with him on Sunday, she'd accepted. It was so kind of him to keep on asking her like this, she couldn't turn him down again. And at least while she was crewing for him in that extraordinary contraption—she couldn't think of the twin-hulled racing machine in the same breath as a yacht like *Lapwing*, for instance—she'd have no chance to think about anything else. Or anyone else.

He called for her at first light, and they walked down together to the hard by the sailing club, and launched the catamaran. Nicola was soaked through before they'd even set sail, but she ignored this. Giles was right, sailing this fast twin-hull was exhilarating. Rewarding, even. And certainly it gave no opportunity whatever for miserable brooding. She ought to do it more often.

There was a brisk wind, gusty and unpredictable, and they had to watch the set of the sails and the wind that came skimming over the water, and go about at the crucial moment. Going about meant, for Nicola as crew, crossing over from one hull to the other, across the netting between them, and the struts and the sheets. Wet, bruised—catamaran-handling was even more bruising as a pastime than dinghy-handling, she found—she seemed to be perpetually lurching ungracefully across from one hull to the other, banging her knees and in constant likelihood of falling in the drink.

Giles didn't find Nicola's action ungraceful. Triumphant at having persuaded her to come out with him, delighted with her company, he was pleased to see her, as he thought, relaxed, happy and occupied in the fresh air. This wind would soon blow all the nonsense out of her head. She'd begin to realise that down here at Halchester was the place to be.

He even wondered if he might give up all thought of the championships, settle for sailing like this with Nicky instead. Good for both of them. Did he have to be so competitive? Now he'd more or less landed his consultant post, should he give up competitive sailing and settle for companionship with Nicky?

Neither of them was in the least prepared for the sight that greeted them as, after a strenuous hour, they made for the harbour again, and breakfast at the sailing club. *Lapwing*, coming in, like themselves, from the open sea, and making for her mooring.

Nicola was astonished. Michael had told her there'd be no chance for a sail this weekend. He had to be in London on Saturday, he'd said, and on Sunday he had to meet Jane's father at Heathrow. But there he was, on board *Lapwing*, and with someone crewing for him, too.

Andrew.

Impossible. She screwed up her eyes against the sun glinting off the waves, and stared again. Still Andrew.

On the opposite tack, the catamaran, with Nicola and Giles gaping, hurtled past *Lapwing*. Michael waved cheerfully.

Giles, though his mind was spinning, waved back with equal cheerfulness. Nicola raised a wan hand.

Andrew, in his turn, produced a quick automatic salute before he turned away. Nicola and Giles. Just as Michael had told him.

Giles started to pray fervently that he'd succeed in

keeping them apart, Nicky and Andrew. Awkward if Andrew appeared in the sailing club for breakfast. It might all come out about Gillian—and how was he going to get out of that one? Hell. When he'd taken so much trouble, and entirely for Nicky's sake, too. He hated lying to her, and he hated seeing her so unhappy, but he'd had to do it. He had somehow to save her from herself, set her free from being torn apart, destroyed. If his efforts came to nothing, it would be Nicky who'd suffer.

Nicola was thrown. First there'd been the spurt of sheer joy that seeing Andrew always roused in her, but followed almost instantaneously by intense gloom. He'd come down to sail with Michael, but he hadn't bothered to let her know. That was how much she counted. What's more, Andrew's face had done anything but light up when he saw her. He'd looked grim. He'd looked, in fact, the way she'd occasionally seen him look in the operating theatre, when all was lost and there was nothing more they could any of them do. No hope left.

Why should he suddenly be looking like that? Last week at Westhampton he'd been his usual self. Today he looked quite different. As if he was in some sort of torment. Could something have gone wrong with his plan to join Gillian? She couldn't, surely, have thrown him over again? For the second time?

Or could she? Would it be just like her? For a moment Nicola wanted to yell across the water, across the fast-widening space between *Lapwing* and herself, yell to Andrew's oblivious back as he stood in the bow, ready to take the mooring, to forget Gillian. '*Here I am,*' she wanted to shout at him, '*ready and waiting and loving you, and only you, as I always have. Forget Gillian.*' She was stopped, not by the fact that he probably wouldn't be able to hear her, but simply because he had looked so unhappy she couldn't bear it. If he needed Gillian to stop him looking like this, then he must have her.

Giles shouted at her. They were going about. She must concentrate.

They had to go about half a dozen times before they reached the hard by the sailing club.

'I'm soaked,' she told Giles, when they had at last dragged the catamaran up on to the hard, and were ready to go into the club for breakfast. 'I think I'll skip breakfast at the club, if you don't mind, and go straight home and change.'

'Right,' Giles agreed thankfully. That was his problem solved. 'You do look a bit damp. Hang on a minute, though. I wanted to ask you. How about lunch at Long Barn?'

'Long Barn?' She was startled, and briefly jerked out of her preoccupation. 'Why? Is it some sort of celebration?'

'Sort of. I'll tell you about it when we're there. So will you?'

Lunch at Long Barn would fill up her day, keep her on the go, stop her drifting about brooding. She could have a shower, some breakfast, and then change for lunch. After that she'd be at Long Barn for an hour or two, and by then this might all seem a silly fuss about nothing. In the meantime she wouldn't think about anything. 'Thank you,' she said. 'I'd like to.'

'Great. I'll pick you up about eleven-thirty—that'll give us time for a walk, and a drink before lunch.'

He left her at her door, and returned to his own cottage to ring Long Barn and book a table. Poor silly Nicky. One glimpse of that bloody Andrew, no more than a casual wave from a passing boat, and she was all to pieces.

The point had come when he ought to take matters into his own hands again. He wasn't going to stand by doing nothing while she ruined her life.

He'd intended to wait until she was over Andrew before stepping in himself. But apparently that would mean waiting until they were old and tired and on the verge of retirement. So he'd act now. This was the psychological moment.

They were so well suited, he and Nicky. They'd have a marriage that would last, nothing like this crazy infatuation she'd always had for Andrew. They'd live here at Halchester, work at St Mark's, raise a family, and sail a boat. It would be a good life. So if he had to tell a few lies along the way, and more or less hijack Nicky into it, what did it matter? All in a good cause.

Anyway, the opposition from Nicky wouldn't amount to much. She'd be glad, if he knew her, to be free of her obsession at last, and settled down with him. What's more, he had this house to tempt her, and Nicky was susceptible to houses.

First, though, he had to tell her about his post. He did this over drinks at Long Barn.

'You've made it, Giles. That's terrific. Oh, of course you were right, we must have a celebration meal.' Even if her own life was a shambles, at least everything was going ahead for Giles. Dear Giles, he deserved this. And if he wanted her to celebrate his success with him, she must put her own problems into cold storage, behave as if life were all gas and gaiters for ever.

'Of course,' Giles was explaining cautiously, 'I don't actually get the job for another year. Not until Bagnold retires.' But he rubbed his hands together almost gleefully, his eyes shone with triumph, and his sturdy square figure emanated a force she'd observed in the operating theatre, when a difficult piece of surgery began to go well, when the end was in sight and, against the odds, he'd pulled it off.

They had wine with the roast lamb and redcurrant jelly, finished it off with a selection of English country cheeses—Double Gloucester, crumbling Wensleydale, a tangy Caerphilly and a creamy Somerset. To add her own contribution to the party atmosphere, Nicola insisted on providing brandy with their coffee. 'We've had our walk, after all, and two hours sailing as well. So there seems no reason why we shouldn't for once indulge ourselves by sitting about all afternoon full of food and drink.' The wine had made her a little more cheerful, and brandy with her coffee might, she hoped, set the seal on her improvement.

Giles was hoping so, too. 'As a matter of fact, I've an appointment later on. I hope you'll be prepared to come with me, provide the woman's angle. A house I want to look at.'

'A house?' She frowned. 'Aren't you jumping the gun a bit?' Giles had always had this streak of rashness, he was inclined to go too far, too soon. She eyed him with misgiving. He sat there, ruddy from the morning's sail and the food and drink. He was oozing confidence from every pore.

She sipped her brandy. To warn him off this house he wanted would be unkind. Anyway, he'd always been able to look after himself—she was the one, not he, who landed in difficulties and had to be hauled back on to dry land.

In fact it was a dream of a house, rambling, with low-ceilinged rooms, ancient oak beams and mellow Tudor brick. Lost along a winding lane that climbed up into the downs, surrounded by smooth lawns tended for centuries past, it had a distant view of the sea.

It was hardly, though, a house for an active, cata-maran-sailing young surgeon working long days and nights in the accident unit, she thought. Very much a family home, for a settled, gardening family who would cherish it, inside and out. Against all her resolutions, against her will, Nicola began to lose herself in fantasy.

A fantasy in which she and Andrew, somehow trans-ported from the Central, though continuing to work there, lived in this lovely rambling old house lost in the downs, living and loving and bringing up a family. So

clear and poignant was the vision that her heart ached
with the pain of knowing that none of it was true.
Andrew was not for her. This dream of a house was not
for her, either. She would never live in these delightful
rooms with him, never have tea in the garden under the
big old apple tree, the wind from the sea ruffling her hair
and the warm southern sun browning her limbs. She
would be earning her living in some city centre, and
Andrew, in California with Gillian, would sun himself
by a different sea.

Shaking off her dreams was difficult, but at last Nicola
forced herself to pay attention to what was going on.

Immediately she found herself in a quandary. Not
unnaturally, the elderly owners of the house had
assumed that she and Giles were househunting together.
If only she'd been listening earlier, instead of mooning
about thinking of Andrew, she might have been able to
slip in a remark that made her own position clear, that
established her place as the female adviser only, no
more, no less. At this stage it was too late to say anything
without producing embarrassment all round. The kindly
owners, evidently sure they'd made a sale—Giles' runaway enthusiasm again, carrying all before it—were
talking about leaving the old house in good hands,
stressing that it was a wonderful house to bring up
children in, hoping that they'd both be so happy here.

Nicola had to clench her teeth and accept it, but she
shot an evil look at Giles for letting her in for this.
Avoiding her eye, he thanked the owners and asked if he
might ring them later? When they'd talked it over.

'Of course, of course,' they chorused. 'You must talk
it all over together.' They waved them off, pleased and
confident, and Nicola tried to wave back in the same
spirit. They'd been so kind and welcoming, she felt
guilty at her deception. Except that it had not been her
doing, but Giles' own achievement. Deliberate?

Warning bells at last began to ring.

Giles had done it on purpose.

So what was he up to?

He drew up in the first parking space they came to, by a gate into a field at the edge of the lane. 'Liked the house, eh?' He seemed full of confidence still.

'Of course I did. It's a dream. But—'

'Thought you would.' He nodded. 'So how about it, then, Nicky?'

'How about *what*?' she demanded irritably.

'How about the two of us setting up house there, eh?'

'But Giles—'

He didn't allow her to go on. 'I know it's not easy for you to give up the idea of Andrew, love. Don't think I don't understand how you feel. But honestly, Nicky, it's gone on long enough. You've got to snap out of it sometime. It's doing you no good, and it's leading nowhere. Why not drop it now, today? Here, this minute. Why not turn over the page and begin again? Marry me, and settle down here, in this wonderful house. We could make a go of it, Nicky. I know we could. You wouldn't be sorry. Not once you'd got used to it.'

She was half touched, half exasperated. In an attempt to avoid hurting him by delivering an outright refusal even to think about his suggestion, she reached hastily for the obvious practical disadvantages. 'But Giles, you know perfectly well I've only got two years at St Mark's. I can't possibly take on marriage and a house here.'

'Oh yes, you can.' His confidence was unimpaired. 'I've got this consultant post—in a year or two, it'll be the same for you. You've already got old Fubbydiddles in your pocket, you'll easily find another post round here. Way I see it, you'll be giving gases round the countryside for the rest of your days.'

The prospect was like the knell of doom.

'So what are we waiting for?' he was asking. 'A house like this isn't going to come on the market again in a hurry. Come on, love—be brave. Turn your back on the past, and step out into the future. With me. It'll be OK, you know.'

Trying to bribe her with a house. And yet, the way he was putting it, it began to seem not so impossible. In many ways he was right. It would be sensible. All the same, how could she go through with it? 'But Giles, I'm sorry, but the trouble is, I—I don't love you.'

He didn't flinch. 'No, of course you don't.' He was almost breezy about it. 'You love Andrew. You can't suppose I haven't grasped that?' He grinned.

Nicola gave him a wavering smile in return.

'But you've got to get over him. You must see that by now. And you're quite fond of me, you know you are. Why not let that do to start with? Rely on me, Nicky. It'll be all right.'

If only she could. 'It's very sweet of you, Giles, to want me to. But—'

'Who dares, wins.'

'Yes, but Giles—'

'Come *on*, love. Be brave. Take one big step into the future, and don't look back.'

'Giles, I—'

'At least think about it. And believe me, I know what I'm talking about. It'd be the best thing possible for you. You've got to start a new life without Andrew.'

Reluctantly she nodded. 'That's true.'

'So why not with me? What have you actually got against the idea, except that I'm not Andrew?'

'Nothing,' she assured him hastily. 'Nothing at all.'

'So why not think it over?' If she did that, he'd win. Or the house would win for him. He was banking on that.

'All right, I'll do that.' It seemed the very least she could promise him.

He seemed satisfied with it, took her back to her own cottage, kissed her—but in a friendly sort of way, on the cheek—and, to her immense relief, left her. She let herself in, and paced the tiny house. Upstairs, down-stairs, into the kitchen, upstairs again, pause at the window and look out across the estuary, pad downstairs again and make circles in the living room. This was ridiculous. Stop it. Stand still. Use your head, not your legs. That she might be running away failed to occur to her.

In some ways Giles was right, she had to recognise it. What stopped her from going the way he wanted was that to do so would be such a final step. What, for instance, if . . .?

What if nothing. She must put Andrew out of her mind and concentrate on Giles. But her uneasiness only grew. Surely marrying Giles, when she loved Andrew, had to be a mistake? Sensible, admittedly, in many ways. But if she didn't love him, surely that ought to be the end of it?

She didn't want, did she, to spend the rest of her days as a single woman, simply because she couldn't have Andrew? If she couldn't have love, she could have companionship. Affection and companionship, and a family—brought up in this sweet house in the downs— and her own job as an anaesthetist, too. Most people would say she had it made. So why not settle for it, marry Giles and begin a new life?

A picture of the house in Harley Street sprang— unwelcomed and unwanted—into her mind. Andrew's living room seemed to stare at her, with the tall book-cases, the comfortable chairs, and the French windows to the roof-top garden.

She fell on to her window seat and howled.

Eventually she braced her shoulders, blew her nose, and took hold of herself. She had to reach some sort of a decision, not sit about bawling like a teenager and feeling sorry for herself.

Staring out of the window across the estuary, she faced the fact that after all her dreams—fantasies was the word, she reminded herself morosely—after all her fantasies of Andrew and herself in *Lapwing*, sailing the wide waters, disappearing, so to speak, into a purple sunset for ever and a day, what in reality happened was that he gave her a casual wave from *Lapwing*'s deck, she gave him one back from Giles' catamaran, and the two boats went about on the other tack. So much for that. And if she tried to kid herself as to any possible reasons why she and Andrew had ended up on different boats in the same harbour, without having been in touch with one another (and what was the telephone *for*?), she had only to remind herself that he had not been waiting for her on the hard, when she and Giles stepped ashore. If he'd wanted to see her, even in this so-called friendly way she'd been selling to herself for months, he'd have been there. To say hullo.

There had been no sign of him. No telephone call from him, either.

So there it was. Giles had been right from the beginning. What she had to do now was face facts, and remake her life.

She was a well-qualified senior registrar at St Mark's, with a consultant post ahead of her. More than time, then, to stop mulling over Andrew, and the transient relationship they'd shared for a few weeks.

Only she didn't seem able to do it. Every cell in her body cried out for Andrew.

Perhaps if she was to speak to him for a minute or two, she'd recover from this desperate feeling of absolute total loss. After that she might be able to settle down, do the sensible thing, and remake her life.

To hear Andrew's voice, even down the telephone, always did wonders for her, so why not simply dial, now, this minute, and speak to him? Once they'd talked, she'd be all right. She always was. The infallible cure. Two minutes with Andrew on the telephone and she'd be back to normality.

As she dialled the familiar number, her pulses began to pound, and her breath quickened.

But the telephone rang on. She let it ring. Long before she replaced the instrument, though, she knew it was no use. Andrew wasn't there. She wasn't going to be able to talk to him.

Probably it was just as well. This was her life, her problem. She was the one who had to face it, and make a decision—and live whatever life she chose. If she chose to marry Giles, she'd be the one to live with him, in that dreamy house in the downs, and bring up a family. So what in the world did ringing Andrew have to do with it? Lucky, perhaps, that he hadn't been there.

CHAPTER ELEVEN

Andrew

ANDREW spent Sunday afternoon in the hospital. Work took his mind—though only briefly—away from that view of Nicola and Giles sailing the catamaran, tacking away from him for ever. His temper was worse than anyone had ever known it. The staff caught one another's eyes behind his back, raised long-suffering brows, and speculated together, the instant his tall and angry back disappeared through the automatic doors, as to what could have happened to upset him.

'He cleared off suddenly yesterday, you know. Said he was going for a sail, his houseman told me.'

'I've never known him so impossible.'

By late afternoon it dawned on him what a miserable Sunday he was inflicting on them all, and he took himself back to Harley Street to consume his own smoke.

To his amazement, as soon as he was there, sanity enfolded him like a comfortable old coat, and for the first time he asked himself what he supposed he was up to. He'd gone down to Halchester to talk to Nicola, and to begin a determined campaign to retrieve her from that oaf Giles Yorke. So why hadn't he carried out his plan? Well, because of what Michael had told him on the way down. So what? For crying out loud. Was he infirm? Or did he perhaps suppose Giles to be Superman?

Why in the world hadn't he stormed in and detached her from Giles? She was his girl, and she had no right to play around with Giles or anyone else. He'd had over twelve hours in Halchester in which to make this plain to her, but instead all he'd done was to belt back to London and the refuge of the Central's wards.

He must have been out of his mind. Nicola wasn't

Gillian, as he'd reminded himself only a day or two ago for the hundredth time. Perhaps he'd been wrong to accept Gillian's departure. Maybe he should have fought that, too. At the time to do so had seemed unthinkable. He had escaped into anger, and walked away fast in the opposite direction. And then with Nicola he'd followed precisely the same course. Why on earth hadn't he asked her, when she accepted the St Mark's post, what her feelings were about the two of them? Did she want him to come down to Halchester and see her?

He'd said nothing. He'd been set on keeping aloof, determined on a policy of non-interference with her career. Looking back, though, he seemed to have been demented. He ought to have told her how much he was going to miss her, and talked to her about their future together.

All right. So he'd been temporarily out of his mind. But he wasn't any longer. The way ahead was clear. He had to tell Nicola how much he loved her.

There was the telephone.

He picked it up, dialled. No reply.

Where was she? Out with Giles, or called to intensive care or the accident unit? He let the telephone ring on, somehow feeling that they were more in touch if he was holding a telephone that pealed out in her sitting room.

Nicola's sitting room. He didn't even know what it looked like. He hadn't the faintest notion. She had been down in Halchester for something like nine months, and he hadn't seen the inside of her house.

Depression rose like a cloud round him. His own fault. He hadn't been into her house because of his own idiocy, that's why. To start imagining now that she didn't want him there, had never invited him because she hated the very sight of him was nonsense. What's more, if she did think anything of the sort, he'd change her mind for her. He'd show her she was wrong.

But what was he going to do this afternoon?

He was going to ring her every half hour until she came home, and when she did, he'd make a date. Simple. Why he hadn't done this months ago he couldn't imagine.

To fill in time until he could ring her again, he reached for the *Lancet*.

The journal, not unnaturally, failed to grip him. He threw it down and began to prowl the house. He plodded downstairs—the lift was switched off for the weekend, as was customary—and leafed through his diary for the week ahead, trying to work out when he could fit in a half-day off to see Nicola down in Halchester. It wouldn't be easy. He'd do it, though.

Restless as ever, he returned upstairs, picked up the *Lancet* again, put it down again. In the mood he was in he might as well be reading the telephone directory. He scanned his bookshelves, looking for something gripping, to make him forget the time passing so slowly. Nothing held his interest.

He went off to the bedroom, showered and changed. That had taken up a reasonable slice of what he might as well start calling the evening, and at last he could have another go on the telephone. Still no reply. Hell and damnation, what was he going to do with yet another half hour to fill? Too early to eat. Not too early to drink, but if he began downing alcohol between every telephone call to Nicola he'd be paralytic before dark.

In default of anything else to do, he went out to the roof garden, sat there on one of his teak chairs, feeling sorry for himself.

This wouldn't do. Perhaps he should sweep up, make the place presentable. Not that he was planning to entertain there. His thoughts look a predictable turn, and to keep them at bay, he began sweeping ferociously. Immediately he felt a good deal better. Energetic and capable, instead of a worrying idiot. He had to smile to himself. Here he was, sweeping his roof garden in the gathering dusk, all because he couldn't get hold of Nicola.

Perhaps it was time to ring her again, he thought hopefully. But when he glanced at his watch, no more than twenty minutes had gone by. He sat down again on the teak chair, leant back and stared at the sky. This, he realised suddenly, was how patients' relatives must feel, sitting about in waiting rooms or outside wards, filling in time somehow, anyhow, until he came through and told them how the patient was, whether he'd come through the operation, what had been found and what the future might hold. They could stand it, though, the waiting, and so could he.

Down below in the street there was a crashing like an old rubbish cart doing its rounds, and for a wild moment of sheer ecstasy he mistook it for the sound of Nicola's old heap of a car. How mad could you be?

It did undoubtedly sound like Nicola's old heap. Ridiculous, it couldn't be. She'd probably changed it months ago, in any case, for a new model. He must be totally out of his mind.

He peered round the trellis, trying to spot the Council rubbish cart, or whatever it was in the road, but he could see nothing to account for the row. Might as well go down and see what it was. He knew of course that it wasn't Nicola, he wasn't so far gone that he truly imagined she had arrived outside the house, but it would do no harm to go down and investigate.

He raced downstairs, jumping the last four treads as one, and opened the front door.

There stood the old heap itself, and round the back of it came Nicola. His own Nicola, at last.

He took her into hungry arms, and held her as though he never intended to let her go. 'I knew it was you,' he told her untruthfully. Or perhaps truthfully. He was no longer capable of working anything out. Except that she was here, in his arms, and that he loved her. For ever.

His arms tightened round her, and she tipped her head back and looked at him with what seemed to be all the love the world could hold. He bent his head and kissed her, tenderly, slowly, cherishing the warmth of her softness held against him, and then suddenly much harder, as excitement flooded them both and their bodies stiffened.

He opened his eyes to drink in the delight of her nearness, and saw at once that she was pale with exhaustion. His heart flooded with a protective love that startled him by its strength, and he pushed his demanding body with all its urgency forcibly into second place. 'Come upstairs, love, and I'll get you something to eat. When did you last have a meal?'

'A meal?' He had bewildered her. She had felt his body stiffen, and the last thing she had expected was that he would begin talking about food or drink. She was, though, she realised with surprise, actually rather hungry. 'Well, I suppose it must have been lunch,' she said vaguely. Lunch with Giles at Long Barn, and his talk of the house. It seemed a world and light years away.

'Lunch?' he repeated. 'And since then you've driven up here? Or did you have lunch in London?' If so, who with, he wanted to shout at her.

'No, I had lunch in Halchester. With Giles, as a matter of fact, and then I drove up.'

With Giles. He might have known it. But then she had set off for London to see him. So much for Giles. What had actually made her do this he didn't know, and didn't much care. What mattered was that she was here, with him, and very shortly he was going to make wild glorious love to her. But not yet. Not bloody yet, he told himself. First of all she was going to rest, while he fed her, and cherished her and looked after her.

He'd begin by carrying her upstairs.

'Hey,' she protested, as she found herself scooped up, iron bands holding her against Andrew's beating heart—rather furiously beating heart, it had to be said, and not unnaturally.

'You're worn out,' he told her, his voice seeming to come from somewhere deep down in his chest.

'Not that worn out,' she said. 'I could have managed the stairs. But I must say this is very nice. Super, in fact. I must get you to do it more often.'

'Any time,' he told her, by some amazing exercise of will-power refraining from panting and puffing, his put-upon body producing the effort he demanded of it, instead of the effort in which it would much rather have indulged. He took her into the sitting room and deposited her on the big sofa. 'Lie back, put your feet up, and I'll bring you a drink.'

Nicola lay back with a sigh of utter content. Never in her life had she been so transported with happiness. Here she was again with Andrew, in his sitting room, on his sofa. Back home, with Andrew. Life held nothing more, or ever could.

She'd done the right thing. It had seemed mad at the time, though suddenly it was the only thing she could possibly do. And it had been right. Here they were, together, and Andrew, there could be no possibility of denying it, Andrew was as pleased to see her as she was to be with him.

She kicked her shoes off, raised her feet on to the sofa cushions, and let her body sag, while her heart sang a triumphant song.

Andrew appeared from the kitchen, and she let her eyes rest lovingly on the broad shoulders she had been yearning for so many months to hold, the tall figure she'd seen in her mind's eye so constantly, and the face that had looked so grim this morning—only this morning? Aeons ago—on *Lapwing*, and now looked so astonishingly young and full of joy. Just as she was full of joy.

He reached her, and it dawned on her that he was holding one of his tall glasses bubbling with what looked like champagne.

'Not champagne, Andrew? Why?'

He watched her and knew he loved her for ever. He spoke hastily, his sentences muddled, blurted out before caution could step in. 'Champagne's the only drink for this sort of celebration, and that's what we're having. I mean I hope we're both going to have a celebration. Will you marry me, Nicola?'

The words she'd imagined so often. 'Any day,' she said surely. 'Of course.' And then second thoughts came, and she regarded him uncertainly. 'But what about Gillian? And California?'

'Gillian and California?' He looked blank. 'What's she got to do with us?'

'I thought,' she said slowly, puzzled, 'you were going to California to join her.'

'Me? Join Gillian? That's the last thing I'd do. Surely you know that?'

Golden phrases. 'I do now,' she said, and sipped her champagne.

'But what on earth made you suppose I'd even think of it? Gillian and I were finished years back—and anyway, what we had—oh, love, it was nothing, nothing whatever to do with what you and I share.' He put a very gentle and immensely loving finger against her cheek, and ran it up and down with tenderness. Touching her maddened him, and yet she was so precious to him that at the same moment this slight glancing contact seemed to be more than he'd ever expected from life until now.

In all their loving, he'd never touched her quite like this before, and Nicola closed her eyes with the joy of it.

She sighed, and he gave her a quick butterfly kiss on each of her closed eyes. She opened them, with the flash of blue light that he loved, that he'd missed so intolerably, and said 'Did you say something about you and

Gillian—that what you had with her was—was nothing like you and me?'

'Of course it isn't.' He stood above her, almost glaring down. 'How could it be?'

She shook her head. 'I don't know. But I thought it was—um—a good deal better.' She was almost ashamed to say it, now she was with him, yet she'd been so certain until now that she'd been no more than a second best substitute.

'Rubbish. Nothing has ever been like us. As for Gillian—that never really had a chance.'

'Not a chance?' Difficult to believe, but delightful.

He shook his head. 'I was a boy, I suppose, and I mistook some rather glorious sex for a lifetime's love. Gillian didn't want love, she's a tough career lady through and through, and if she did want it, she wouldn't get it from me, in any case. Because I happen to love you.'

'I honestly thought she'd always come first, you know. Everyone seemed to think so,' she added apologetically, since her thoughts now appeared so blatantly untrue. 'And when you met her again, that evening—on your *birthday*, too—I was certain you were both getting together again. So I thought I'd better take the St Mark's job, and clear off out of the way.'

Andrew was transfixed. 'Nicola, do you mean to tell me—' he broke off. 'I suppose it must have seemed a possibility, but all the same, why on earth—' He broke off again. He knew why she had said nothing. He saw it all. She'd tried to creep away and hide, to keep her desolation to herself. The past shifted and slanted, and he could see the explanation for so many actions that had at the time angered him. Worried him, too. It had been Nicola, though, who had suffered far more than himself. And he'd brought it on her, by stupidity and carelessness. Because he hadn't troubled to explain about Gillian.

Because, to be honest, he hadn't wanted to explain about Gillian. She had been his failure, to be pushed out of sight, and forgotten, whenever possible.

'I've made us both unhappy,' he said. 'I ought to have told you all about Gillian from the beginning. I'm going to tell you now.' He sat down in the easy chair, the coffee table between them, so that he could only talk, not lose himself in touching her, and told her exactly how it had really been for him over the break with Gillian. It didn't come easily to him, even now, when it was all in the past and hardly, he thought, mattered any longer, it still didn't come easily to him to bring it out, the story of his hurt over Gillian. But he made himself tell Nicola, and told her straight from his heart, unloading on to her all his muddled pain and loss and anger. When he came to the end he said, a little angrily, 'So now you know. That's how it was. I took it far too seriously, of course. But at the time it was rather nasty. And I took it about as badly as I could have, and handled it hopelessly. I ought to have told you before. Anyway, it's finished. That evening I met her, I realised, I don't even like her very much.'

He didn't even like her very much. And that was the truth, Nicola was sure of it now.

Andrew stood up. 'It's you I love, and I'm sorry it took me so long to realise how different what you and I have is from what came earlier. I've been so bloody slow, love, and you've paid a price.' He was close to her again, and he touched her cheek again, in just the way he'd done before, very gently and tenderly. 'Forgive me if you can. I do love you so much.'

Nicola's eyes blazed love back at him, and she took his hand in her own. They clung together.

'You are going to marry me, aren't you, love? In spite of everything?'

'In spite of nothing,' she assured him. 'Of course I'm going to marry you.' She gave him a radiant smile, that turned his bones to water.

'Thing is, I don't know how to live without you. I'd be finished if you said you didn't want to.'

'I wouldn't have dreamt of saying anything so dotty. But I'm not in the least sorry you can't live without me, because it's been horrid down at Halchester without you. I haven't liked it a bit, and I was afraid you didn't mind at all.'

'Not mind? I'll show you how much I mind.' He almost fell on top of her as she lay on the sofa, but his censorious commanding self, ruling from his mind and not his body, took over, and instead of hurling himself on top of her, he stepped inflexibly back. He was going to look after her, wasn't he? So far, all he'd done was deposit a glass of champagne into her not unwilling hands, and sit down and pour out his soul. He'd promised her a meal, and sex would have to wait until after he'd fed her.

He decided first to lighten the mood for both of them—not that this was difficult, since happiness was sparking out all over him, and he felt much more like a boy of nineteen than a hardworked surgeon of nearly forty. 'We are engaged,' he announced. 'Tomorrow I shall go out and buy you an extravagant ring. Ostentatious and in thoroughly bad taste, a vulgar great thing for you to flaunt around St Mark's to show everyone you're mine.'

'Chauvinist pig,' she said dotingly. 'I love you. I love you so much I shall probably expire from happiness any minute.'

'Have some more champagne instead, while I fix you some food.' He poured champagne into the tall glass, and then forced himself to unglue his feet from the floor next to the sofa, and trod firmly off to the kitchen to examine the contents of the refrigerator. Nicola was here with him, and she loved him. They were going to be married.

She was also quite plainly worn out, and he was going to look after her. Take care of her. Making triumphant love to her would have to wait for a while. Not for very long, after all. Just until she'd eaten.

On the sofa in the sitting room, Nicola sipped champagne, and checked her watch casually to see how many hours of this blissful existence she had ahead of her. To her shocked disgust her watch informed her the time was already past eight o'clock. She had to be back on call for intensive care from midnight, and to drive back to St Mark's in the old Beetle would take over two hours. She had only another hour with Andrew.

He appeared from the kitchen with a plate of sandwiches. 'Smoked salmon,' he told her. 'And let me pour you some more champagne, love.'

'No, I can't. Sorry. I've only got an hour, and then I'll have to drive back. So no more champagne. Black coffee, more likely.'

Andrew was staring at her. 'I thought you'd be staying the night.' His voice was hollow.

She remained cheerful. 'Doesn't matter.' She patted his hand. 'I feel quite different now I've seen you.'

He took hold of himself. 'Love, no way can you set off and drive back to that place. You've only just got here. You'll be worn out.'

'All I have to do is keep off the champagne and I'll be fine.'

'Listen, you're not going to drive that old heap down the motorway tonight.'

Nicola munched smoked salmon and wholemeal bread, nodding vigorously. 'Oh yes, I am. I'm on call from midnight, and that's it.'

'Ask someone to stand in for you.' He gestured towards the telephone. 'Ring up and see.'

'I can't possibly. I took off for London without warning, and all I did was ring poor Dominic from a telephone box at the motorway service station and con him into covering for me. I swore I'd be back by midnight at the latest and take all his night calls in return.'

'Hell. There it is, then.' He glanced at his watch. 'Coffee, then, and we'll be on our way.'

'We? Andrew, you—'

'You're not driving down there, and then taking all the night calls for the accident unit and this Dominic character too. You drove up, I'll drive you back.' He sighed sadly. 'Not in the Porsche, either. You'll need your car down there during the week, so I'll drive you down in it, and get the train back.'

'But—'

'No trouble. And I'll have that bit more of you.' He kissed her.

'If only I could stay.' She clung to him. 'Not a chance, though. And I honestly don't think you ought to have to drive me back—especially not in the Beetle. You'll loathe driving it after the Porsche.'

'True enough. But I see no alternative.'

'Perhaps I could manage without it for a week, and you could use the Porsche.'

'You need your car to get to and from the hospital, you said so when you first went there. Now, look, get back on the champagne and stop arguing.' He poured her another fizzing glass, and handed it to her. 'I'm the one on the wagon. And I'm the one in for a spot of telephonic bullying, too. So while I talk to the troops, you can lie back and drink champagne.'

She smiled at him. 'Being engaged to you is the most satisfying experience.'

'What's more, it goes on and on, you'll find.' He ruffled her hair and made for the telephone.

Half an hour later, with two brimming mugs of strong black coffee inside them, they were on their way. Nicola was dreamy, acquiescent, dazed with love—at St Mark's they'd hardly have recognised crisp Dr Lancaster— while Andrew was unusually dogmatic.

At eleven-forty-five precisely Nicola let him into her little harbourside cottage, brimming with pride and delight. Here he was, in her own home at last, just as she'd imagined so many hundreds—or more likely thousands—of times. She hugged him joyfully and made for her own telephone. 'I'll just put Dominic out of his misery, and then we'll have some tea, shall we, and I'll show you round.'

'First time I've heard it called that,' he told her with a broad grin.

Nicola snorted, and turned to the telephone. 'Dominic? Nicola. I—'

'Aha. So you've made it. And just as well. Here, duckie, we have all hell well and truly let loose.'

'I'll come in.'

'You have a pile-up from the town centre. A nice example of drunken driving after the pubs closed. Injured pedestrians, and a nightwatchman going on duty knocked off his bike. Fractured femur. The accident theatre's booked for him for twelve-thirty. He's going to be a tricky gas. Elderly—he's a pensioner—shocked, and I don't like his tracing. I'll meet you in the unit and fill you in, as soon as you can make it—I've the main theatre getting ready for an emergency perforation. If you hadn't booked in by midnight plus one I was going to ring Ogilvie.'

'Thanks for hanging on. I'm on my way.'

Andrew took her into reassuring arms, though he felt more like cursing and throwing things. 'I heard,' he said. 'Typical accident unit Sunday night. Not to worry. Clear off and relieve Dominic, and I'll explore this place myself and make some tea. Climb into your bed, too. Don't hesitate to wake me when you return, will you?' He held her to him briefly. 'Take care, love,' he said, and waited in the doorway while she started the Beetle, reversed it, and drove off.

In the accident theatre, as well as the old nightwatchman, there was Giles, steaming with irritation. Not only had he been dragged out just as he was thinking of going to bed, but he'd been informed Nicola was not available until midnight, if then, and he might have to operate with her chief giving the anaesthetic. He'd been put out. Where in the world had she gone, without a word to him? A hideous possibility jolted him—surely he couldn't have driven her too far, with his talk of forgetting Andrew? Surely not. Nicola was sensible and stable, not a neurotic teenager. Even so, he'd been worried half out of his mind, and to find her fit and well, though it was an undoubted relief, jerked him into a disagreeable fault-finding mood. 'Where on earth have you been?' he snapped, as soon as there was a spare moment.

'Up to London.' She was short.

'London?' He shot an astonished glance at her, blankly, and then jumped to a conclusion. The correct one. 'You've not been up to see Andrew, I hope?'

'As a matter of fact, yes.' Nicola was airy. 'I had supper with him.' Smoked salmon and champagne, and we got ourselves engaged, she thought. But she wasn't going to say more at present. He could make what he liked of what she had said. Let him sweat it out.

On the way down to Halchester, she and Andrew had uncovered the details of what had to be regarded as Giles' plotting. Andrew, of course, had been less astonished at the new light thrown on Nicola's oldest friend than she had been. Both of them had been a little ashamed that they had allowed him to throw them into such misery, but Nicola had decided, she'd told Andrew firmly, not to have it out with Giles. 'It was awful of him, and I can still hardly believe it,' she'd said as they crashed noisily down the motorway, 'but we've come through in spite of him, and now it's in the past. As far as I'm concerned it can stay there for ever.'

She was still of that opinion. Apart from which, she was certainly not going to raise what had happened with

him over the operating table. Nor was she going to make
the first announcement of her engagement in the accident theatre at one o'clock in the morning, when she was
supposed, in any case, to be there to look after this poor
old man with the broken thigh. Giles could think what he
liked.

Over his mask his eyes were hot and angry. 'You need
your head examining.'

'Thanks very much.'

Round the table under the glaring lights eyes scrutinised first Giles, then Nicola, and then met across the
patient, eyebrows lifting, amazement and curiosity
growing by the second. This was supposed to be the
happy couple on the very eve of marriage—they'd even,
rumour had it, found a house.

Nicola could feel the speculation growing, while the
probing eyes darted and crossed as if they were at a
tennis final rather than an emergency operation. She set
her lips and ignored them. Just as firmly she pushed to
the back of her mind her own happiness and the glorious
memory of Andrew and herself together in the Harley
Street house. She was back on the job, and tonight the
challenge she had to face was the need to bring this frail
old man through the surgery on his fracture. She looked
across at the simmering Giles, and said 'I'm not really
keen to have the patient very deep, though I know that
poses a problem.'

Giles at once seized the chance to attack. 'For God's
sake, Nicky, use your head. How can I operate on his hip
without adequate muscle relaxation? Tell me that.'

'I know it's a bit of a knife-edge decision.'

'Knife-edge? Huh.' It was an explosion, and eyes
crossed again. 'It does so happen, may I remind you,
that I am the surgeon using the knife in question. Any
operating tonight is being done by me, not, as you
appear to imagine, by you. Your job is merely to
have the patient suitably anaesthetised so that I can

work on him. I suppose you are actually using a muscle relaxant?'

Surgeons were often trying and given to outbursts of temperament. Nicola, as she nearly always did, kept her cool. 'Certainly he's had a muscle relaxant. Ten minutes ago, to be precise. But neither Dominic nor I—we've both examined the patient, and consulted over him, and—'

'You mean you skipped off to London, instead of staying here on the job.' Giles hated Nicola for first of all worrying him stiff by her disappearance, and then, to crown it, tearing off to bloody Andrew when she was meant to be considering his own perfectly serious proposal of marriage. He had every right to be furious with her. And now she was back at last, she seemed able to do nothing but put obstacles in the way of the proper exercise of his surgical skill. This was more than he could be expected to put up with. 'What you mean is that Dominic had to see the patient for you, and now you're simply repeating what he told you.'

'Certainly Dominic saw the patient first, as I wasn't here,' Nicola agreed silkily. Nothing could throw her tonight. She was too surely based in happiness for Giles at his worst—and undoubtedly this was his worst—to seem of any more importance than a five-year-old in a tantrum. 'But then we saw him together—about half an hour ago—and went over him thoroughly. So, yes, in a way you're quite right, in the circumstances I do have the backing of Dominic's considered opinion on this point. We both feel there's a danger of heart block—there's a long PR interval in his tracing that we don't care for at all. If his heart does stop, I've the pacemaker ready, of course. We're fully equipped and prepared. But I'd rather avoid it if we can, naturally. So I don't want him too far under if it can be avoided. How long do you think you're going to be?'

Belatedly, Giles took hold of himself. He had to

postpone the showdown he was determined to have with Nicola, get on with this hip surgery. No doubt there might be something in what she was saying, even if she had lifted her opinions at second hand from Dominic. Taking a deep breath and enunciating his phrases with clarity and the sort of undertone that might have been expected from patience on a monument in person, smiling bravely at grief and forgiving all who had injured her, he said, 'I have to spend time pulling the displaced hip joint fragments into better alignment before I can begin to insert the pin.'

'The sooner the better,' Nicola responded, adjusting the gas mixture, watching the patient, and plainly locked into the needs of the moment.

Giles was even more irritated. She could ignore him and devote all her attention to the job in hand, as if he, her oldest and truest friend, thinking only of her well-being, was no more than any anonymous surgeon doing a hip repair. However, Central training—reputed by some to be the best in the country, if not the finest in the world, at last told, and he transformed himself into that same anonymous surgeon, and got on with his hip repair. 'Let me know at once, then, if you're not happy about the patient,' he remarked impersonally to the opposite wall, 'and I'll ease up until you're no longer worried.'

'Cardio-respiratory function is satisfactory at present,' Nicola said, with a detachment equal to his own, and addressing the foot of the table.

Step by step, Giles worked methodically—if morosely—until he was able to pin the fractured pieces of the neck of the hipbone together. 'There we are, then. That's it.'

'Praise be. The sooner this anaesthetic is out of him the better. I'll change to oxygen and a little CO_2 now, to wash it out.' Giles might have finished, but Nicola had a long haul ahead of her, she knew, seeing the patient through from the recovery room and back to intensive care.

At one point she thought the old man was going to arrest, but she succeeded in bringing him through until his heart settled again. However, she didn't dare leave him, though she took five minutes to have a coffee and ring Andrew. It was seven in the morning, though, before she was able to park the Beetle outside her cottage again.

Just enough time in hand to drive Andrew to the station to catch the London train.

At the door he met her, took her into his arms. 'My poor love.'

She hugged him joyfully. 'Did you find everything? I expect you did. I'll take you to the station.'

'For the train at seven twenty-five. I know. I rang the station. I was just wondering—got your house keys? Good. I was just wondering if I ought to have rung for a taxi.' They settled themselves into the old heap, Nicola reversed and drove off. 'But I had it worked out that no matter how busy you were, you'd send a message if you weren't going to be able to drive me to the station for the first London train.'

'That's right. I would. I ran it a bit finer than I meant to, though.'

'How's the patient?'

'Surviving. That's about as far as one can go, though. He nearly arrested on the table, and then again in intensive care—oh, I told you.' Weeks ago, it seemed now, that she had rung him from the hospital to tell him not to wait up for her, she was in for a long haul. Months ago, it seemed, that she'd left Halchester for London, thinking she must be mad yet knowing she had to do it. She had to see him. And she'd been absolutely right. So much for listening to Giles.

She'd done far too much listening to Giles. He'd given her the wrong advice. Deliberately, it seemed, and that he'd deceive her like that would never have crossed her mind. Well, it should have done. She'd been slow and gullible, and she and Andrew had both paid a price for it. However, they'd come through.

She drove into the station forecourt. 'I'll drop you off and park while you get your ticket. Three minutes in hand.'

He kissed her quickly, like a commuting husband. 'On my way. Take care.'

'You, too. Look after yourself, for me.'

He kissed her again, and then strode across to the ticket office.

Nicola leaned out of the car window. 'I'm so glad I came up to London yesterday,' she yelled after him.

He turned on his heel. 'Me, too,' he bellowed, before disappearing into the booking office.

Nicola arrived on the platform just in time to wave him goodbye as he leant out of the carriage. Her eyes misted as the train pulled out and she lost sight of him. She'd never been happier in her life.

CHAPTER TWELVE

Harley Street Again

RUSH AND TEAR and hasty station partings became the pattern of their meetings. Snatched nights in London or Halchester, often interrupted, often cancelled. They stopped driving up or down, the train was quicker, and allowed them to sleep throughout the journey. When they weren't able to meet, they ran up enormous bills on the telephone.

At St Mark's their engagement was the latest sensation. What a turn-up for the books, they marvelled, though Dominic proclaimed that ever since the Westhampton conference he'd known there was something in the offing. Hardly anyone believed him.

At the Central everyone noticed Andrew's change of mood, but only Leo went so far as to ask Andrew what was up. 'Bin mooching round f'r months, y'r face as long as an old boot. Suddenly it's the flowers that bloom in the spring, tra la. What's up?'

Greatly to his surprise, as he had intended to keep his marriage plans a secret from the hospital, Andrew heard himself confiding to Leo the information that he and Nicola had decided to marry. 'If we can ever succeed in fixing a week off at the same time.'

'Delighted to hear it. Great girl, Nicky. You and I, perhaps, better get together, have it out with our diaries, eh?'

Andrew agreed that this would be an undoubted help, and that afternoon they sat in Leo's room, their diaries before them, and played around with dates. Andrew rang Nicola, and with a bit of juggling on Leo's part—and Dominic's, too—they eventually fixed a date. A little to Andrew's surprise, Nicola was adamant that she wanted to be married in London. She'd like her Central friends round her, and a reception in the Harley Street house.

'Suits me,' Andrew said. 'Can't think of anything I'd like more.'

'You can go to Moyses Stevens again, as well,' she said wickedly. 'And lay on some food and drink for the occasion, while I swan up at the eleventh hour.'

He grinned. 'Will do.'

'I'm afraid I shan't be able to come up this weekend, though. Not after treating Dominic like that on Sunday. He had a perfectly frightful evening, rushing about between the accident unit and the general theatre.'

'I don't quite see how I can get down, either,' Andrew told her reluctantly. 'We'll just have to try hard for the one after.'

Leo watched Andrew put the telephone down with sympathetic eyes. 'Know how y' feel.'

'Can't be helped.'

'Y' know what? Why doncha forget about weekends? Try for mid-week. Bound to be quieter on the accident unit then—and I don't mind covering f'r you for a coupla days mid-week.'

'You're right, of course. I'll take you up on it. Thanks.' Typical of Leo, Andrew thought, to see the obvious solution to their problem.

At this point it occurred to Andrew that another of Leo's characteristics was that he invariably knew exactly where to obtain anything needed, from a jubilee clip to an *haute-couture* ball gown. He had a network of former schoolfriends, students and ex-patients, all apparently doing splendidly in useful corners of commerce, industry or hospitals world-wide.

'Leo, I want to buy Nicola a really super ring. A bit lavish and out of the ordinary. I haven't the faintest notion where to start—never gone in much for buying jewellery in the past.'

'Izzy.' Leo reached for his address book, read out an address and telephone number.

Andrew took it down. Hatton Garden. It would be.

'Give 'im a call first on the blower, tell 'im what you just told me, and he'll 'ave a few knuckledusters looked out for you to see.'

In principle, Andrew knew exactly what he wanted. A stone to pick up the heavenly blue of Nicola's eyes. Izzy found him a sapphire with diamond shoulders, at an alarming price that he paid without so much as a blink. Nicola quivered visibly when he presented her with it, on the two days off in mid-week that Leo had also organised for them. Her reaction, though, was as nothing to that at St Mark's, where they were shaken out of their minds.

During those two short days, Andrew and Nicola managed to do almost everything she had dreamt about through the long months of loneliness. They walked along the shore path in the dawn when the tide was out, and the track seemed lost among the marshes, and again late at night, when darkness had fallen and it was high water, they trod the streets round the cathedral and its Georgian terraces, they shopped together for their supper in the supermarket on the hard. They made love at last in Nicola's bedroom overlooking the estuary, made coffee and drank it folded up in the window seat, watching the sailing.

A fortnight later, Andrew came down to Halchester again for Wednesday and Thursday. They had dinner with the Ogilvies, went to Long Barn for a fabulous lunch, Nicola's eyes, as Andrew had known they would be, as blue as her sapphire, and liquid with love. Eating the amazing Long Barn food—though it was wasted on them, they registered only each other—they planned their wedding. In another month, they'd be married and on their honeymoon.

'Only four weeks,' Nicola said, her heart in her eyes.

Andrew took her hand in his—not in the least in the manner he'd taken it across the breakfast table in Hampstead over six years earlier. 'Four weeks, love, and you'll be mine.' His eyes danced. 'Then you'll find out what I'm really like. I shall beat you every second Tuesday, just to make sure you know your place.'

'I know my place all right,' Nicola told him. Her mouth quirked, and she explained in somewhat basic terms exactly where she meant.

'Right. Let's get out of here, go back to that cottage of yours and spend the afternoon in bed.'

'Let's. I must do some food shopping on the way, though—and save enough energy to cook supper. A pity, but there it is. The Adversanes are coming.'

He sighed. 'We have marvellous friends, and I value them deeply. I just wish they'd all get lost for a month or two.'

'Do you think, on our honeymoon, we'll actually be able to wangle the odd day alone? Or will some horrible coincidence put us in the same hotel as a group of American surgeons on the way home, or a crowd of Australian anaesthetists en route for Europe, whom it would be unthinkable to avoid?'

Andrew was thoughtful. 'It could easily happen. We ought to have booked ourselves a desert island.'

'A pity we can't just hole up in Harley Street and simply pretend we're in the South of France, while we soak up the sun on our own roof top.'

'Would you like that?'

'Love it. But it wouldn't work—they'd be sure to find out at the Central, and you'd have endless calls, asking you to just look in and see this patient, or meet so and so who's passing through.'

Andrew frowned. 'I don't know, it's worth thinking about, anyway. Now, about this evening—before we leave here, are you sure you wouldn't rather we brought Mike and Jane here for a meal? I could book a table when I pay the bill. It would save you a good deal of bother.'

'I know it would.' Nicola was suddenly clothed in embarrassment. 'It's just that—that—well, it's silly, I know, but I have so longed for us both to be entertaining together in the cottage.' To her fury, she went scarlet.

Andrew was touched, not so much by what she said as by how she looked saying it. Determined and red-faced and about ten years old. His unexpectedly defenceless love, the cool, poised and self-assured Dr Lancaster. 'Of course we'll have them in the cottage, if it's what you want. Let's go shopping for food for the Adversanes.'

As well as food, they bought armfuls of copper chrysanthemums in the market. Andrew lighted a fire of logs, and when Jane and Michael arrived, the long room smelt of flowers and woodsmoke. Nicola's veal and tomato casserole was a huge success, the wine they'd bought in Halchester went with it perfectly. After the meal they sat on in front of the fire, drinking Andrew's delicious brew of strong coffee, remembering libellously funny episodes at the Central right back to their student days, and collapsing into breathless paroxysms of laughter. Well after midnight, Andrew and Nicola went out into the cool night air to see the Adversanes off, afterwards strolling in the dark along the harbour path. The next morning Andrew caught the early train for London.

A fortnight later, Nicola spent two days in Harley Street with him, their last meeting before their wedding. She went back to the boutique in Great St Anne's, and bought another sizzling dinner dress and a soft blue velour track suit for lounging in the roof top garden in the autumn sun. Her wedding dress was taken care of—sent down by her mother, after much telephonic argument over design and styling. Her mother's intention, in Nicola's eyes, was for her to be married in something like a crinolined ball gown, with a twenty-foot veil of Honiton lace that had belonged to her

great-grandmother. Nicola vetoed this instantly, maintaining against all pressure that she wanted a dress she
could go on wearing in the evenings. Her mother, after
forwarding a selection of pages pulled from back num-
bers of *Vogue* portraying models six foot tall garbed in
frills and furbelows from head to toe, finally came to her
senses and discovered a slim tunic of heavy ivory silk
with a glittering chemise top, beaded and embroidered,
and a matching jacket cut in that season's short line with
a high collar and wide cuffs in winter ermine. What it
could have cost Nicola didn't dare think, but she adored
it.

On the final evening of her stay in Harley Street, they
had dinner with Leo and Judith.

Judith wanted to know about the wedding dress. 'It's
come, has it? And you're pleased with it?'

'I am, yes. I can't bear to think what it cost, but it is a
dream. My mother seemed determined to be truly extravagant—I think it was her way of enjoying my wedding
at second hand. She and my stepfather aren't coming,
they'll be in America. Some conference he can't possibly
miss.'

'Your father's coming, though?'

'So he says.' Nicola wasn't counting on it, though. 'It's
in his diary, at any rate,' she said, with an undertone of
sarcasm not lost on Judith.

'Parents in medicine are murder, aren't they?' she
commented sympathetically. 'By the way, *my* father is
fearfully pleased about you and Andrew—has he by any
chance thought of telling you so?'

'He sent me a very nice little note. I thought it was
sweet of him.' She had been surprised that Robert
Chasemore had even thought of writing to her.

Judith, though, was persistent. 'Ah,' she said darkly,
'but did he really sound as if he was *delighted*?'

It had been a typical Robert Chasemore letter, formality itself. 'Well,' Nicola began, 'Actually I thought it

was terribly nice of him to bother at all, and—'

'There you are. I knew it.' Judith heaved an exasperated sigh. 'Dad is quite unable to communicate. But I'm his daughter, and I know what goes on behind that stony facade. He's truly chuffed about you and Andrew, and he's already planning a super post for you when you finish at St Mark's. He'll have it all lined up, probably before you even return from your honeymoon, if I know him.'

'But—'

'Ask no more. My lips are sealed. Dad's being a bit devious, and I mustn't blow the gaff. But if I know my old man—and I do—it's in the bag.'

'Judith, do you really mean—no, I'm not going to ask you to say another word about it, but do you really mean that I can secretly count on coming back to the Central this time next year?'

Judith nodded. 'And Dad's schemes always work,' she added. 'That's how he is. And that brings me to another point. Leo has a scheme about your honeymoon.' She leant forward, her tawny hair glinting in the light, and expounded the plan at some length.

'What an absolutely perfect idea,' Nicola breathed. 'I can't think of anything I'd like better. You are geniuses.'

'Oh, good. I insisted on putting it to you—those two men would just have gone ahead and laid it on, regardless. You know them, they have all the answers. But if you like it, I'll give them the go-ahead.'

'Like it? I love it.'

'Right. It's on. Leo, she likes our scheme.'

Leo, reliving that morning's cholecystectomy with Andrew, blow by blow, looked up. 'Told you she'd go for it,' he said briefly. 'Could've gone ahead and fixed it, would've bin OK.'

And so at last on a golden October day, Nicola and Andrew held their wedding reception in the big attic living room, its windows open to the roof garden.

Champagne flowed, the food—supervised by Judith and prepared by Leo's London housekeeper, Mrs Noakes—was meltingly delicious. Both the room and the garden, stacked by Moyses Stevens with dahlias glowing in every shade from blush pink to garnet, were like a vision of heaven.

Nicola, in her lovely dress and jacket, and a rope of fabulous pearls sent by her father, was a vision of heaven, too, Andrew thought—or, as Leo put it, 'a right sight for sore eyes, and I'm takin' a kiss off the bride stat.' He gave her his famous leer, kissed her well and truly, and then grabbed Judith to kiss her even more thoroughly. From that moment the reception took off.

Apart from Dr Ogilvie and his wife from St Mark's—Dominic, standing in for both Dr Ogilvie and Nicola, had necessarily to remain in Halchester—the celebration was attended almost entirely by staff from the Central. Nicola's father had had to cancel at the last minute, as he was flying out to Kuwait for an emergency operation. He had despatched Securicor with the pearls, and that was all the contact they had with him—Andrew had been furious, maintaining that Nicola's wedding should have come before surgery, but Nicola herself hardly cared. She had fathers galore today, all self-appointed stand-ins, longing to cherish her and see she lacked nothing. Even Leo was pushed aside by his father-in-law, Robert Chasemore designating himself father of the bride, *in loco parentis*, though Dr Ogilvie jostled him for the post, and both of them found themselves outclassed by the doyen of general surgery, Lord Mummery, up for the day from the country and insisting, as ever, on playing any leading role that was on offer.

Eventually, though, Nicola and Judith extricated themselves from what had become indistinguishable from any other hospital party, and slipped downstairs for Nicola to change. 'Do you think they'll cotton on to the fact that something's up when they see me in my track suit instead of an outfit by Chanel?' Nicola enquired, as she climbed out of ivory silk and into misty blue velour.

'No, why should they?' Judith retorted. 'No one in their senses these days would travel from Heathrow in anything from Chanel—a track suit is far more practical and comfortable—my mother always travels in one when she comes over from the States. Hurry up, though—Jeremy went off to collect Leo's car as soon as we came down here.' She chuckled in a pleased sort of way, and almost pushed Nicola through the door. 'You look great,' she assured her. 'But go *on*—we're into the split second timing bit now.'

Andrew and Leo were waiting at the lift, and hustled the two girls in. The doors closed, and they descended to the ground floor, while a rabble of well-wishers hurtled down the stairs, flight after flight, to mill round them in the hall, yelling and hurling confetti in all directions.

The mob erupted with them on to the pavement, where Andrew's Porsche waited at the entrance. And this was where Judith's split second timing came into its own.

As they stepped across the pavement, Jeremy Moorcroft, Andrew's registrar, drew up alongside in Leo's big orange Mercedes. He stepped out of the driving seat, Andrew stepped in, while Leo hustled Nicola into the passenger seat. 'There y'are, ducks,' he said comfortably. 'Reckon we can still outsmart the troops when we give our minds to it, eh?' He gave her a glance of malevolent triumph as he shut the door on her.

Back on the pavement Leo turned to his houseman, who had been prominent among the confetti-throwers. 'Now you'd better organise a team to put Mr Ritchie's car in order,' he snapped. 'I shall expect to find it in my parking space at the Central in pristine condition by—

let's see—by four-thirty at the latest. I've a patient to see out at Epsom, a domicilary with a GP, and I want a respectable-looking car to use for that. I leave it in your hands.'

'Pipped at the post,' his houseman was irrepressible today. 'I suppose I might have known it. I'll see to it, sir—may I have the keys?'

Leo handed them over, and turned to go indoors, winking at Judith. Andrew's Porsche, as they had foreseen was a disgrace. Two separate groups of well-wishers had been at it, one of aesthetically-minded romanticists (mainly female) and another of rebellious juniors (mainly male). The car had white silk ribbons, and white daisies and chrysanthemums taped to the bumpers and festooned round the windscreen. It also bore a number of placards announcing 'Just Married', with various witty and lewd additions, and an assortment of old boots and tin cans.

While their juniors were removing all this, Andrew and Nicola were driving smoothly out of central London in the Mercedes, through Kensington, over Hammersmith Bridge, across Barnes Common and on towards Leo's house by the river at Richmond.

They had the keys, and let themselves into the spacious hall, then walked through into the large drawing room overlooking the garden and the river. Here a table laid for tea greeted them, an electric kettle at the ready.

'Tea,' Nicola said thankfully, sinking down on to the sofa. 'What I want more than anything in the world at this moment.'

Andrew chuckled. 'Leo and Judith don't miss a trick, do they?' He plugged in the kettle, sat down by her side, and took her hand. 'You looked wonderful for your wedding, Dr Ritchie,' he said. 'And you look wonderful now.' He kissed her lovingly. 'I trust everything was to your liking.' She had arrived in Harley Street only the night before from St Mark's.

'I've had exactly the wedding I would have chosen, at Harley Street, in the garden with all my friends from the Central—even Lord Mummery thrown in, which I certainly never dreamt of. That's a tribute to you, of course. And the food was perfect, and the drink, somehow everything ran on oiled wheels—and I didn't have to lift a finger.'

'All done by remote control. Leo played his part—the main ideas originated with him—but the real management came from Judith. A slick organiser.'

'Terrific. And talking of Judith, drink up. As she reminded me when I was changing, all this is planned to split seconds. So swallow your tea fast and keep an eye on the landing stage.' Outside the French windows, the wide garden sloped down to the riverbank. She glanced at her watch. 'Nearly time.'

Leo and Judith were at this moment travelling upstream in their launch. They'd tie up at the landing stage at the end of the garden, Andrew and Nicola would step aboard, Leo and Judith would retire up the garden to the house, while Andrew took the launch downstream again, down to Westminster Pier, where a hand from Tough's Boatyard would take over the launch, while Andrew drove Nicola back to Harley Street and their honeymoon in their own home.

'And here they come, I think,' Andrew said. 'I'll get on down and take their lines.'

Hastily Nicola swallowed the last of her tea. 'I'll come with you.'

In the garden, dusk was falling, and lights already glowing from the opposite shore.

'Don't tie up,' Leo shouted from the deck of the shining launch. 'Just 'ang on for 'alf a mo', while we come ashore, and we'll take 'em from you. Then y'can get straight away—the tide's just on the turn, so you'll 'ave it with you down river.'

Judith came and took the stern rope from Nicola. 'All right?' she enquired.

'All right? I should think so. Bloody well perfect, in fact. Thanks for everything—especially the tea, which just about saved my life.'

Judith nodded. 'I thought it might. Champagne is wonderful, but one can have enough of it.'

Nicola laughed. 'I never thought to hear myself agreeing with a statement like that, but how right you are.'

'Get on board—we'll get bawled out if we stand about talking. You'll find the man from Tough's at Westminster, and he'll show you where the Porsche is parked—don't worry, Leo made them clean it up. It's quite presentable.'

Nicola hugged Judith fervently. 'Thanks so much for everything.' She turned to go on board, to find Leo in her path.

'Don't I rate a hug too?'

'Leo, you've been marvellous.' She hugged him with immense enthusiasm, and he hugged her back, lifting her off her feet.

A shout came from the launch. 'Unhand my wife, blast you. And see to the head rope, that's what you're supposed to be there for, or I'll be in midstream before Nicola's on board.'

Within two minutes they were cast off, and cruising downriver, the big diesel throbbing under their feet. Andrew had done the navigation with Leo a couple of nights earlier, he told Nicola. 'Basically, though, it's simple. Just keep to the middle of the channel. But we ought to check each buoy as we go, and if you could keep an eye on that, then I'll have all my attention for other craft.' He gestured at the open chart.

'Will do,' Nicola agreed. She gave a faint shiver, as the night air caught her. 'Judith said something, when I was changing, about there being an anorak on board,' she remembered. 'I wonder whereabouts—'

'Just behind you.'

'Oh, I see. Good. What a super colour—is it Judith's?'

'No. Yours. Meant to be your colour.' Andrew was abrupt.

'It is, too. Good grief, it's heavy. It's fur-lined. Andrew—what on earth is it? You can't call this an anorak. It's beautiful.'

'The outside's proofed. It has a hood.' He was laconic, but his eyes were probing, as he slanted quick glances towards her, and then back to the river ahead.

Nicola stroked the fur. 'It's fabulous, whatever it is. The outside feels like silk, proofed or not, and the fur inside is silky, too.' She squinted down at it, trying to gauge the colour in daylight—at present she had only the glow from the dash and their navigation lights. 'It seems to be a sort of blue-grey, and the fur too.'

Andrew came clean. 'Sapphire mink—or so Leo alleges. You like it?'

Nicola shrugged herself into it. 'I love it. It feels terrific—and, you're quite right, it's so practical. It *is* an anorak, in a way—but what an anorak. Sapphire mink. Wow. Never did I expect to live to see the day I'd be wearing mink. I shall wear it and wear it, I assure you. Everywhere. In bed, probably.'

'I'd like that. In fact, I'll keep you to it.'

'That won't be difficult, I assure you. It'll quite likely be impossible to part me from this gorgeous garment, the most super thing I've ever possessed.'

'It's reversible, by the way.'

'Oh, so I can drift around with the mink outside, can I, if I want to?'

'That's right.'

'My God, I'd forgotten about checking the buoys— I've been much too excited.' Snuggling into the fur, she peered around. 'Where on earth are we?'

'We've passed the London Apprentice and Syon

House, left Kew Gardens behind. Just coming to Chiswick Bridge. Then it'll be Hammersmith Bridge again, after that Putney, and back to central London. With the tide under us like this, it won't take too long.'

'I don't care how long it takes. We're on our honeymoon, and I love you.'

'I love you.'

Sailing home down London's river.

They were approaching Chiswick Bridge, and Andrew's eyes were alert and on the water again. He wore the closed expression familiar to her over the operating table, and she studied the lines of his face with, at last, possessive love. His dark hair was ruffled in the wind, his deepset eyes scanned the river, the wide mouth set, while the illumination from the instrument panel caught the cleft in his chin. Her husband, Andrew Ritchie. At last they belonged together. An overwhelming ache of love swept through her, and she caught her breath.

His left hand came off the wheel, and his arm was round her shoulders. 'My dear wife,' he said.

Doctor Nurse Romances

Amongst the intense emotional pressures of modern medical life, doctors and nurses often find romance. Read about their lives and loves in the other two Doctor Nurse titles available this month.

THE LEGEND OF DR MARKLAND
by Anna Ramsay

Totally forbidden territory for a girl engaged to be wed — that's Dr Bram Markland with the roving eye and lethal lifestyle. Just when her fiancé is injured and needing her, Staff Nurse Helen Westcott finds that Markland is planning to step in and do a smooth take-over…

SURGEON IN WAITING
by Clare Lavenham

Having lost his memory and broken his arm in a car accident, aspiring surgeon Chris Felgate takes a temporary job in a group practice while he recovers. And there he meets Nurse Nicola Craven — who seems to know more about him than he does himself!

Mills & Boon
the rose of romance